"Solid plotting, believable townsfolk who exhibit realistic behavior in the presence of murder, descriptions of rural America in the 1930s so genuine you can feel the grit on your hands and a gruff, likeable hero who says what he thinks."
—*Los Angeles Times*

"Adams has a fine ear for dialogue and his characters' voices ring incredibly true. And his prose? Lean as a Depression-era paycheck." —*Star Tribune* (Minneapolis)

"Adams creates a remarkable cast of memorable minor characters; the restless wind across the desolate plains whistles through their voices and their lives." —*Booklist*

"There's nothing sappy or sentimental in Adams' depiction of his small-town characters. The secrets they hide are as dark, the violence they mask is as ugly, and the passions that guide them can become as lethal as any that drive the suspense in a modern mean-streets crime novel." —*Alfred Hitchcock's Mystery Magazine*

"Harold Adams writes in prose as spare as the dustbowl days in which he sets his Carl Wilcox series." —*South Bend Tribune*

"No one since Agatha Christie has found more menace or mendacity in village life than Adams— he knows what evil lurks in the hearts of men."
—*The News & Observer* (Raleigh, N.C.)

W9-BEI-648

LEAD, SO I CAN FOLLOW

The Carl Wilcox Mysteries

LEAD, SO I CAN FOLLOW

A CARL WILCOX MYSTERY

Harold Adams

Walker & Company
New York

First published in the United States of America in 2000 by
Walker Publishing Company, Inc.;
first paperback edition published in 2000.

Published simultaneously in Canada by Fitzhenry and Whiteside,
Markham, Ontario L3R 4T8

Library of Congress Cataloging-in-Publication Data

Adams, Harold, 1923–
    Lead, so I can follow : a Carl Wilcox mystery / Harold Adams.
      p. cm.
    ISBN: 0-8027-3336-0
    1. Wilcox, Carl (Fictitious character)—Fiction. 2. Private investi-
gators—South Dakota—Fiction. 3. Corden (S.D. : Imaginary
place)—Fiction. 4. South Dakota—Fiction.
I. Title.

PS3551.D367 L43 1999
813'.54—dc21   99-055556
ISBN 0-8027-7596-9 (paperback)

Series design by Mauna Eichner

Printed in Canada
2 4 6 8 10 9 7 5 3 1

This one is to John Mayor,

close friend for over

forty years.

I also want to acknowledge once more my debt to Barbara Mayor, who has been my personal editor and supporter through every book I have had published.

LEAD, SO I CAN FOLLOW

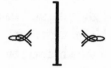

It was about an hour before dawn, when even the mosquitoes had retired. There was no wind, not an owl hoot, a cricket's creak, or a farm dog's howl. After crawling out of my sleeping bag and relieving myself a dozen yards away from the tent, I ambled back and was just about to duck inside when a shot from the top of the bluff east of our island froze me in a crouch. As I began to straighten up, there was a yell, then a scream that seemed to last an age, finally stopping abruptly.

Inside the tent Hazel's voice called anxiously, "Carl?"

I opened the flap, ducked inside, and told her what I'd heard, while scrambling into my duds.

"What're you going to do?"

"Take a look."

"How'll you know where to look in the woods?"

"If somebody went over that bluff, he likely wound up on the railroad tracks."

"You can't be sure of that."

She was probably right, but there was no chance of more

sleep, and I couldn't just let it ride. Hazel rolled out of her sleeping bag and began pulling on clothes.

"You stay here," I said. "No point in both of us wandering around like damn fools."

"No way," she told me, squirming into her slacks. "I agreed to love, honor, and obey only when it made sense."

"I missed that part of the parson's line!—"

"Here's your flashlight," she said, handing it to me. "Lead, so I can follow, you're bigger than I am."

Mostly I was just a little heavier, but it didn't seem worth arguing.

The moon was at quarter, and the Milky Way glowed across the clear sky. We raced over the beach to our canoe, which went into the water with little more than a gentle scraping on the fine sand. She scrambled in first, then I pushed it clear and hopped into my position at the stern. We crossed the narrow channel separating our tiny island from the mainland in a dozen strokes. After pulling the canoe up, we stopped and listened. Except for echoes of frogs croaking in the small lake to the west of the river, there wasn't a sound.

We scrambled along the edge of a narrow spring stream that poured icy water down the bank and passed the place where we'd filled our water jug the last two mornings. Then it was a steep climb through brush about fifteen or twenty feet before we reached the railroad bed.

As we approached the tracks, the earth began trembling and a train whistle shrieked. We emerged from the dense brush and halted. There was nothing unusual in sight until the first reflection of light from the oncoming train showed a lump on the tracks toward the south on my right. I started running. By the time I reached the body, the lights were direct enough to reveal bright pulsing blood and the whiteness of a shattered bone.

"Look out!" yelled Hazel.

I reached the body, grabbed an arm, and dragged the broken mess clear of the tracks as the steam engine thundered by with its whistle screaming.

azel and I had decided to be married before the end of August, and despite Ma's disapproval of what she considered our unseemly haste, she sent out invitations, worked over the feeding arrangements with Bertha, the hotel cook, and got the minister from her church to handle the ceremony. It went off just fine.

We had actually spent more time planning our honeymoon than the wedding. My first idea was to work a deal with Pinkerton, the guy I'd painted my biggest sign for, to rent one of the lake cottages he owned near Aquatown, but Hazel knew a friend from her teenage years who'd taken her canoeing on the St. Croix River between Minnesota and Wisconsin, and she'd been convinced that was the most romantic area in the world. So we finally wound up with about a ton of camping equipment, one cooler full of beer and wine, and another of food, which barely packed into the trailer I hitched to my Model T. We rented a canoe at a place on the river on the Minnesota side near Taylors Falls.

Canoeing was all new to me, so Hazel had to show me the ropes—or, more like it, how to handle a paddle and not to stand up unless you wanted to swim quick. It turned out very okay. We went into the water up by Indeville, launched the canoe, and spent what seemed like a week packing our gear and vittles into it. Since I've been a traveling man most of my life, stuffing luggage into limited space is one of my best-developed talents, and a canoe is easier than a trunk to work on if you keep the balance in mind.

The first couple minutes out on the water ended all of my reservations about the idea. The water was smooth and tinted almost red, not the clayish look of the Red River of the north, but more like red wine. The banks were lined with trees and rare stretches of sandy beach, the river twisted so you seldom saw water more than half a mile ahead, and we moved easy, light, and quiet. I learned to watch Hazel from the stern, and when she switched sides for paddling, I'd switch in rhythm to the opposite side. We saw gulls and goldfinches overhead and around the trees, a couple mudhens at a channel leading to a lake, and once a male deer, stepping daintily through the brush on our right, then freezing at the sight of us. Suddenly he was off, his white tail bouncing while his horn rack seemed to float, and he vanished in the deeper woods.

Hazel had assured me she had never gone canoeing with her ex-husband on this river or any other. He was not an outdoorsman. His favorite space was in a bed or on grass, anywhere he could get laid, and the younger his partner the better.

We spotted a small island to our left on a relatively straight stretch of water flowing south and pulled over to have lunch. At both ends there were stretches of beach, the center was well covered with soft maples, and on a sandy spit upstream we found a dense growth of young willows where goldfinches and song sparrows hung out. We climbed a bank about a yard high to a grassy clearing almost dead center that was flat and clear enough for our tent. After eating and cleaning up we explored a bit, wading across the shallow water on the east side and coming up on the steep bank beyond, where a small, sparkling spring trickled through tall grass down to the river's edge. I cupped my hands and tested the water. It was cold and clear.

Back on the island it didn't take long to locate a level spot, put up the tent, and get settled in.

Hazel wanted to fish and began casting off the low, sandy beach point on the south end of our island, while I dug a small pit for our campfire, gathered wood to burn, and put a match to it. Later in the afternoon the first train chugged along the tracks beyond our view, half way up the eastern heights. It was obviously a freight, since we could hear the boxcars rumbling by long after the engine passed. A few moments later a whistle signaled its approach to Indeville, something like a mile or so north of our campsite.

Hazel caught one bass and two northerns, one too small to keep, and we had a fine fish dinner with fried potatoes and a salad she made with fresh tomatoes and lettuce. I took care of the clean-up afterward, and by then mosquitoes began coming out, so we retreated to the tent and had a nightcap of crème de cacao, topping it all off with a great wrestle on our bedrolls.

It looked like this was going to be the perfect honeymoon.

The shot and scream from the bluff sort of changed the prospects.

After the caboose light had disappeared, I worked my flashlight over the body at trackside. The face was too bloody and smashed to recognize if it had been Lincoln's; the body was dressed in blue jeans and a denim shirt. Both were splattered with blood and stained with track dirt. His white tennis shoes were strangely clean.

I checked for a pulse or some sign of breathing and found none.

"The engineer must've seen the body," said Hazel, "and you pulling him clear. Why didn't he stop?"

"He probably figured it'd be quicker if he went on to town and sent back a doctor."

"So what do we do?"

"Hang around and keep the crows away."

I wandered some, trying to find some way to climb up and check the takeoff point, but the rocky cliff offered no promise nearby, and eventually we sat with our backs to the corpse, waiting for somebody to show up while we gazed down toward the St. Croix River, which began to shine in the early morning light.

It was nearly five-thirty when we heard something coming from the north, and in a few moments a handcar with two riders wheeled into sight. The slim man in back stood pumping the handle; his partner, a short and stocky young man, sat in the front, facing us as they approached.

The handcar rolled to a stop a few yards from us, and the hand pumper jumped down and came forward, his eyes darting from us to the body and back. He was tall and straw-haired, with deep blue eyes under overhanging brows. His wide, thin-lipped mouth had wrinkles at the corners that seemed to stretch it beyond real.

"I'm Deputy Dewey," he said, "and this is Doc Fancett. What happened here?" The tone was not accusing, it was almost casual.

I explained, beginning with our reason for being on the river. While I talked, the doctor, who had evidently spotted the body even before getting off the handcar, took only a glancing look at Hazel before heading over for his examination. He was a compact man, younger than any doctor I remembered seeing, and wore a tweed suit that looked a little big for him. He knelt beside the body, paying no attention to the rough gravel against his knees, and his hands moved gently over the bloody mess before him.

"Lemme see your wallet," said Deputy Dewey.

I handed it over. It didn't take him long to examine a ten and four ones, plus a card with my name and a home address in Corden, South Dakota.

The doctor announced that the victim was dead.

"Any identification?" asked the deputy.

"That's your department."

The deputy turned back to me. "You search him?"

"No."

He went over to the body, searched through the pockets, and came up with a quarter, a nickel, two pennies, and a dirty white handkerchief. No wallet or car keys. He stood up and asked me to turn around, frisked me, then turned to Hazel.

"I never went near him," she said.

The deputy's wide mouth turned up at the corners, and he showed a good set of even white teeth in a grin. "Okay. The sheriff's coming in a boat to follow up. He'll want to talk with you back in town. Where's your camp?"

I told him, and he said fine, we'd go down so he could look around while Hazel stayed with the doctor. She said no thanks, she was coming with us. She didn't want to be around that body. Dewey grinned again and said it was okay with him, if the doctor didn't mind. The doc dug out a pipe and tobacco pouch from his jacket and settled down, perched on a railroad tie.

The deputy stayed behind us, and we made short work of the descent. When we reached the canoe, he got in front, facing me. Hazel parked in the center, and I took over the stern and paddled us to the island.

The sun was just making it over the forested hills downstream by the time we disembarked and walked up to the campsite. I tried to imagine what impression it gave Deputy Dewey as he looked over the tent and our campfire layout with the small portable grill and the blackened coffeepot sitting on a board nearby.

"How about I fix breakfast?" Hazel asked.

The deputy thought that was a fine idea and followed as she walked to the tent and started getting bacon and eggs from the cooler that stood near the entrance. I began scrounging up kindling.

e had finished eating and were starting on second cups of coffee by the time a powerboat came around the distant bend, heading our way from the north. The glassy-smooth river reflected the deep blue sky until the wake of the approaching boat turned it into flickering ripples from bank to bank.

Two men observed us in silence from the motorboat. The man in the center seat was a heavyweight who was hunched over, staring at us, from the moment we could make out his features. He looked mad. The guy in back by the motor sat straight, looking over the bow as though he might be picking his way between icebergs. Deputy Dewey put down his cup, got up, and moved along the sandbank toward them. Soon I could see the man in the center had gray sideburns showing slightly under a straw hat that shaded his wide nose, thick eyebrows, and round face.

The boat's bow scraped gently on the sand, and Dewey moved down to pull it up far enough to let the men step out dry.

"I'm Steiger, the county sheriff," said the heavyweight as he climbed out and moved toward us beside the fire. "How long you been camping here?"

"Since yesterday—about noon."

The guy who'd been running the motor looked across the pool between our island and up at the steep bank beyond. He was the oldest of the lawmen facing us, near my height, but leaner and turning gray. He had the look of a South Dakota farmer, underfed and overworked.

"The engineer of the freight that passed this morning says he saw a guy pull a bloody body off the track up there. Was that you?" demanded the sheriff.

"Yup. Heard a shot, then a scream, went up to see who was in trouble, and found the guy on the track. I figured he fell or was thrown off the cliff above there."

"You're not supposed to mess with a body of a murdered man."

"I figured if I didn't, the train would fix it so you'd have no idea what happened. Besides, I wasn't positive he was dead when I pulled him clear. Would you have left him?"

He didn't bother to answer that and asked for our identification.

"I've already seen it," said the deputy. "His name's Carl Wilcox, he's from Corden, South Dakota. This is his wife, Hazel. They're honeymooners."

The sheriff ignored him and went through my wallet thoroughly, then demanded to see Hazel's purse. She went into the tent, walked back, and handed it over. He examined the contents elaborately, setting everything out on the blanket we had spread near the fire, and asked how we happened to pick this area for our canoe trip. Hazel explained about her friend's recommendation. He asked for her friend's address, and looked wise when she admitted she didn't have it on hand or in mind.

After he gave our things back, Hazel offered them coffee. The short guy's eyes lit up, but the sheriff said hell no, this wasn't a damned tea party, it was a murder investigation.

First he wanted to know what I did for a living. He wasn't impressed with my sign-painting claims and only looked ready to sneer when I told him I'd done a couple hitches as a cop in Corden and worked with cops on murder cases in half a dozen South Dakota small towns. He asked where we had been married and let me know he intended to check everything I told him.

Then he asked, scowling at me, if I'd searched the body after pulling it from the tracks. I said no. The deputy told him what he'd found, and what was missing. They both stared at me awhile.

Eventually the sheriff gave up on me, and I offered to take them across the channel between our island and the riverbank in my canoe, since the water was too shallow there for their motorboat and they wouldn't want to wade in their clothes.

The sheriff obviously didn't care for me doing any favors, but he grunted and went along when his deputies headed for my canoe. I suggested that Hazel stay in camp, since five of us would be an overload. He vetoed the idea, letting me know he didn't trust leaving either one of us alone to maybe hide evidence.

"Hell," said Dewey, "he had at least an hour to hide anything between the time the train went by and I got back with Doc Fancett."

"So? Maybe he was too lazy to come down and take care of things and then climb back up here to look innocent when somebody came snooping. Let's go."

We all managed to get in the canoe and make it across. The climb didn't seem either as steep or high as it had in the earlier dark, but everybody was puffing by the time we got up to the railroad bed. The sheriff wanted me to point out exactly where I found the body, and we were able to spot blood on the ties where it had landed a few hours back.

Doc Fancett asked, without any evident sarcasm, if it would be asking too much if Deputy Dewey delivered him back to town on the handcart. The sheriff managed to look apologetic and told Dewey and the other deputy to load the body on the cart. A moment later the two live ones and the accompanying corpse left.

Then the sheriff had me tell my story again, stalked around the territory once more, and finally said we'd go back to the island below.

Back in the camp the sheriff went through all our equipment and, with his silent deputy, poked around the island, not finding anything useful. The sheriff kept muttering to his deputy, how come there was no wallet in the victim's pocket. I suggested maybe whoever sent him over had stolen it first. The sheriff gave me a dirty look, but after stewing a few seconds, he finally gave it up and told us we'd all go back to town in his boat and then he'd check things above.

We rode with Hazel and me sitting on the front seat facing the sheriff and his man. Nobody talked. In Indeville's city hall we sat in a meeting room while the sheriff went for a powwow with a woman who had cleaned the dead man's face up so we could take a look to see if it might be familiar. I doubt it would have been recognizable to its mother.

The sheriff finally made a couple calls I suggested, one to Corden's cop, Joey Paxton, and another to the chief in Aquatown. I got the feeling it broke his heart a little that both of those men made it clear I wasn't a likely villain for his current case. It would be so nice to put the finger on an alien for this job, but now he had to look over the home folk, and he didn't like it.

He sighed and said the obvious place to start was at the top of the bluff, where it must have begun. When I asked if he'd let me go along, he considered it for a second and to my surprise agreed. It didn't seem out of the question to me that he figured having an outsider who was something of a witness would be a good distraction for people he had to question. Hazel said she'd find the grocery, get us some supplies, and meet me at the café for lunch.

Everything was negative from the start. The house nearest to the murder site was a good forty yards from the bluff edge and probably fifty feet north of the place where the body had evidently been pushed or thrown off. Deputy Dewey had figured out where the body went over, not by any visible signs at the top but from the point of landing below. The edge, we saw, was covered by crabgrass and dandelions, which gave no clues. The sheriff and his man wandered the entire area, searching for the missing wallet or any other clues, and came up empty.

After a lot of wandering, gawking, and muttering, the sheriff led us toward the nearest house, which he told me belonged to Cole Bacon. It was like most other houses in the district except it had a light brown paint job instead of the usual white, and the lot was broader than most. Our approach must have been spotted by the occupants; even before we reached the door, an old man pushed the screen open and met us on the path in front. He was gaunt, stoop-shouldered, and shiny bald, with pale blue eyes and half glasses low on his sharp nose.

When the sheriff said we had to talk, he led us through the tiny vestibule into a small, cozy living room with old but well-preserved furniture. He immediately sat down in a big, well-padded easy chair in the far corner, waved us to the matching couch, and asked, "Well, what's my wife done to bring down the sheriff and his posse on us?"

"We got a real problem, Cole. Early this morning a man went over the cliff near here. Looks like he was shot and fell, or got tossed to the tracks."

"I didn't do it," said the old man, "and besides, it was an accident."

The sheriff scowled. "Goddamn it, Cole, this is no joke. Now, did you or your wife hear a shot before dawn?"

The old man, still grinning, said Yes, he had. Somewhere around four A.M. "When there ain't anything up but bakers, screech owls, and rats."

"Hear anything else strange?"

"Heard a car, but that wasn't too strange—though I'll admit we don't hear many that time of day."

"You look out?"

"Nope."

"Your wife hear anything?"

"All she claims to hear at night is me snoring. That's probably a lie—she can't hear me talk during the day, so why'd she be sharp-eared at night?"

"When you heard the car," I asked, "did it take off fast?"

The old man looked at me, shrugged, then asked the sheriff, "Who's this?"

"Wilcox. Him and his wife were camping on the island down below, just beyond where the body landed. He heard the shot and a scream. Did you hear a scream?"

The old man shrugged again. "There was something else—not too clear."

"How come you didn't look out?" I asked.

"Because it was darker than a witch's left tit and I couldn't see anything. How come you're all of a sudden the sheriff's sidekick?"

"He was the one who first found the body, and besides, he's been a cop in South Dakota," said Steiger, "had some experience with killings."

"I thought they only killed pheasants in South Dakota."

"There's a lot of that," I admitted. "Some fish, too. Only they don't shoot them much."

The old man grinned at me. I asked if he had any family besides his wife living here with him.

"Why you ask?"

"Maybe they heard or saw something."

"She didn't. That's my granddaughter. Sleeps like the dead—and late."

"How old?"

"Kat's nineteen."

"His wife's name is Katarina," the sheriff told me.

"That's right," said the old man. "Our granddaughter's named after her grandma. When she was little we called her Kitten, but now it's always Kat."

I asked if we could talk to her. He said no, she wasn't up yet. If we wanted, she'd come around city hall before lunch. He'd bring her in. To my surprise the sheriff bought that, and we left.

At city hall the doctor who'd been looking over our specimen gave the sheriff his report. It boiled down to death by a broken neck, combined with brain concussion. No, he'd found no signs of a gunshot wound, let alone a bullet or buckshot.

"Were you able to clean him up enough so we could have a couple people try to identify him?" I asked.

"Yes, but he'll still be a hell of a mess. It's going to be damned hard on any relative or friend, having to examine what's left."

"How old you figure he was?"

"Somewhere near twenty. No birth marks or significant scars. His front teeth were shattered by the impact—he must have landed face first—but you can tell he's had his wisdom teeth pulled at the bottom. The nose was smashed, and you'll have a sweet time trying to get decent fingerprints—he must have had his hands in front of his face when he hit the train bed."

"You figure he was alive when he started the fall?"

"It seems likely. There's no signs of him getting hit by a bullet or buckshot."

I asked Steiger if he really expected Kat would show up, and he said of course.

That sounded like more faith than good sense, but it seemed futile to argue it any, and I promised to come back after looking up my wife. He said fine.

Hazel was sitting on a bench in front of a variety store, watching the shortage of traffic passing by a quarter of a block from city hall. The bright sun made her dark brown hair glow and brought out the gold in her eyes. After my report she said she bet the victim was somebody Kat knew. I agreed.

It was a quarter to noon when a Model A Ford driven by Cole Bacon appeared and angle-parked in front of city hall. A young blond, sleek as a show cat, stepped out, casually glanced our way, closed the car door firmly, and walked inside alone.

"Well," said Hazel softly, "isn't *she* something?"

got up and walked over to the car where the old man sat, lighting a Lucky. He glanced at me and grinned.

"She's a looker, ain't she?" he said.

"Must take after her grandmother."

His grin broadened. "Not a lot. Actually she gets it from my side of the family. I guess you ain't exactly partners with our sheriff yet—or was it his idea you hang around out here and grill me?"

"Fact is, I never believed you'd deliver your granddaughter until you showed up. Whose idea was it for her to talk with him alone?"

"Hers. She's independent as a hog on ice."

"You figure the guy killed was a boyfriend of hers?"

"I figure *you* figure he was. Don't seem likely to me. She ain't been around town long enough to pick up any new guys."

I dug out my fixings and rolled a smoke. He watched my hands.

"You told the sheriff this morning that Kat lived with you—but now you say she hasn't been around long. Is she just visiting?"

"You got it right. She goes to the University of Minnesota. That's in Minneapolis. Just home for the summer."

He asked me to step back, shoved the door open, got out of the car, and arched his back, saying it was too hot inside. Then he squinted at Hazel, still sitting patiently on the bench nearby. She watched us with a smile as we approached.

"Your lady?" asked Cole.

"Uh-huh."

"How'd you rate a knockout like her?"

"Charm."

"I didn't figure it was looks. How'd you come to pick this dude?" Cole asked her after being introduced. "You could do a hell of a lot better."

"I had a handsome one before. It taught me to look deeper."

Cole grinned, sat down on her right, and asked how come we picked this river for camping.

"Because when I was in my teens I canoed near here with a school friend, and I think it's the most beautiful river in the world, so it seemed perfect for a honeymoon."

"Ah, in this case looks was enough, huh?"

"I'm beginning to wonder."

Old Cole's grin faded, and he glowered at the sidewalk a moment.

"Do you think your granddaughter will recognize the dead man?" Hazel asked.

Before he could answer, we saw the sheriff and one of his deputies come out of the courthouse with Kat and start walking our way.

Kat glanced at Cole with her deep blue eyes, ignoring Hazel and me, as they passed in front of us and moved on.

"Know where they're going?" I asked Cole.

"The doctor's office. That's where the stiff is."

I tried to guess whether his word for the murdered man reflected a conviction that he knew and despised him, or was just an attempt to depersonalize the victim.

"You know if she was going with some guy at school?" I asked.

"She had a string of 'em. Nothing deep—she claims."

"You don't sound convinced."

He waved his big hand casually. "With women, you never know."

Hazel asked him what Kat was studying at the university, and he shrugged. It wasn't a subject that interested him, or at least that's what he wanted us to think.

"Did she plan to teach?"

"It's more likely she went there to find fellas. Ones around here aren't good enough for her."

More questions from Hazel loosened him up a little. Kat had gone to a local grade school, then to high school in Chippewa Falls when her parents moved there. It seemed her father had been a traveling salesman who peddled paint for a Minneapolis manufacturer. Recollections suddenly brought Cole's grin back.

"Ever hear the slogan, 'Blood Makes Good Paint?' " he asked.

We both shook our heads.

"That's who he worked for. The Blood Paint Company. They got took over by the Glidden outfit a bit ago, but that's what their cans showed on the side when he was peddling their stuff."

"So what happened to her parents?" I asked.

"Well, her daddy had a booze problem. One night he raced a train for a crossing and lost. Wife was with him. Both goners." He shook his head. "That was the summer after Kat was a sophomore in high school. We just took over from there. Her boozy dad left enough money in insurance to take care of school expenses, and she's spent the last two summers with us, between semesters."

"She go with any fellows around here in the summer?" asked Hazel.

"Oh yeah, but nothin' heavy, you know? Mostly she makes fun of the local boys. Don't any of 'em read enough books or play with a band."

"She get mail from any fellows she knew in college?"

He shrugged. "Ask my wife. I don't pay attention to the mail. Don't get nothing but bills."

Kat appeared alone in the entry at the side of the corner building north of us and began walking slowly our way. Cole got up, and so did we. The granddaughter looked pale, and her mouth was grim, tighter than when she'd passed before. Her nose was narrow, her cheeks high, and she had a tough chin that didn't quite fit the rest. I guessed a smile would change the sullen look, but suspected it would be a while before I'd see that.

She told her grandfather the sheriff wanted him to come and look at the body. He scowled and took off. She turned her blue eyes on me, and suddenly the chin didn't look tough at all. "You must be Carl Wilcox," she said.

Mostly when people say something like that to me, it sounds like an accusation. From her it was like a compliment.

"Yeah. And this is Hazel, my wife." It was the first time I'd ever made that announcement, and I wondered why I hadn't said "wife" before the name.

Kat's eyes took Hazel in, and I got the distinct impression she was surprised, but she only smiled and came back to me. "Dewey says you risked your life to pull the man's body off the track. Why'd you do that for a total stranger?"

"It didn't seem that close to me—and it was just possible he might still be alive. Fact is, there wasn't time enough to think about it all a lot. Did you know him?"

"I'm not positive." She shook her head and took a deep breath. "The face—I suppose you saw it—it was so, well, shattered. I couldn't make myself keep looking at it. And a body on a table isn't anything like seeing a person standing, you know? You can't judge the height or the build or anything. It's just awful." She plunked down next to Hazel and stared into the street.

We let her think awhile, and then her grandfather came ambling back to join us. No, he said, he hadn't recognized the body, figured he was a stranger. Kat turned back to me. "The sheriff says the railroad engineer told him you barely got out of the way in time to keep from getting killed. You scared him about to death."

"It wasn't that close."

"Well, it was close enough to make him think it was. He said you were quicker than a cat and crazy brave."

"I've got another question. What time did you get home last night?"

She gave me a tolerant smile. "A little after midnight."

Her grandfather confirmed that.

"If you wouldn't mind too much," I said, "we'd like to come out to your place for a short visit. We wouldn't hang around long."

Cole scowled, but Kat put her hand on his arm and said that would be fine. "Whatever you say about your part in this," she told me, "I'm very impressed. I just can't get over it."

"Why?" demanded Cole.

She looked at him with a frown. "Because he risked his life to try and save a man he'd never seen before. Not many'd do that. I can't think of anyone I've ever known who'd have even bothered to climb that hill with the notion of helping someone in trouble in the middle of the night, when he was on his honeymoon."

"It must be some honeymoon," growled Cole.

"Please," his granddaughter said, putting her hand on his forearm, "don't be rude."

"Okay," he said, "let's get in my car, go home, and have lunch. Katarina number one will be tickled pink, I'll bet. Always loves company."

On the way to their house I asked Kat how come she knew Hazel and I were on our honeymoon. She said the sheriff had told her. It was a thing that seemed to interest him a lot. "I think," she said with a grin, "that he envies you about enough to make him sick."

K atarina the First was bigger in all directions than her husband Cole or her granddaughter. She wore a striped dress that fit her like a circus tent. Cole introduced Hazel and me, and gave her a quickie on how I happened to be involved. She took it all in, examining us with dark brown eyes and a smile that showed her slightly gapped teeth, and started making chicken sandwiches while we sat at the kitchen table, drinking strong coffee from thick mugs.

The grandmother asked Kat if she had recognized the dead man.

"I don't think so." She shuddered. "The face was so broken up, it was impossible to tell what it had been like before the fall. I couldn't stand looking at it."

"So how come you didn't just say it was a stranger?" asked Cole, scowling.

She shrugged. "It was just impossible to say anything positive."

"You leaving it in the air like that, it makes cops suspicious."

She shrugged again, but didn't argue.

When Hazel asked what courses she'd been taking at school, Kat looked startled, as though surprised this woman could talk, but after a second she said she was majoring in English lit and minoring in French. Hazel asked if she intended to teach, and she said yes, probably, if something else didn't come up.

She didn't elaborate on that, and I guessed maybe she was thinking of marriage to somebody.

We learned that Grandma Katarina had taught country school for three years before marrying Cole, and her stories of experiences with kids had fascinated her granddaughter when she was young. It was all woman talk from then on, and when we finished our coffee and sandwiches, we left.

"I think the granddaughter knew the man killed," Hazel told me as we walked back to town.

"So do I. But why's she not saying?"

"I'm not sure. There was something going on between her and Cole I couldn't figure. Maybe she just can't admit, even to herself, that it might be a friend."

We went back to city hall, and I talked some with Sheriff Steiger. He made it plain he wasn't about to connect the death with any locals—he figured it was some sort of scrap that came about between tourists, and politely let me know he'd have one of his deputies give us a boat ride back to our camp.

The deputy turned out to be Dewey. I never learned if that was a first or last name.

Hazel suggested we buy some ice before heading back, and Dewey took us to the local ice house, where we bought a twenty-five-pound chunk and got a canvas bag to carry it in. Once in the sheriff's boat, I noticed that while Dewey worked pretty hard at acting like he was giving all his attention to the river, his blue eyes kept flicking for quickies of Hazel. That didn't bother me—if he hadn't, I'd have wondered about him.

"You ever had a murder around here before?" I asked.

"Not for sure," he said.

"What's that mean?"

"Well, in mid-May there was a suicide that looked pretty fishy. Guy named Nate Pryke."

"Nate who?"

He grinned and spelled it. He had said it as though it were Pricky, but admitted it was supposed to be pronounced *pry-key*. "The night he died, he'd been drinking at the beer hall in Foxton and went home alone. His wife was off to Eau Claire, looking after her sick pa. A guy who's done some work at the Pryke farm came to the house in the morning and found Nate in the basement. From the look of things, Nate had gone down into the storm collar, sat on a bench, and shot himself through the forehead with a bolt-action, single-shot Springfield loaded with a long rifle .22 shell. Blew his brains out—or enough to do the job. Some folks couldn't quite believe it was that simple. Especially since his wife, Carmen, had been doing a lot of running around. But her pa backed up her alibi, and that was it. We couldn't come up with a likely suspect because his wife didn't have any special boyfriend anybody knew about, and there were no brothers or other kin that might've felt like doing her a favor."

I asked if Carmen had their only car for her trip, and he said yes. Nobody had seen anyone else around, but then the farm was remote, so who'd see if there was?

He was still talking about the Nate Pryke affair when we pulled up to the island, and the subject died while we hauled the ice and the other stuff Hazel had picked up to our cooler and reorganized the contents.

Before taking off, Dewey made a little tour of the beach with me while Hazel started a fire for our evening meal.

"I guess," he said, "if I was you, I'd keep a good watch tonight.

Whoever tossed that guy over the cliff might not be too tickled about you poking into this thing. You're kind of vulnerable here. Might be smart just to pack up and go back to town."

That had already occurred to me, but I wasn't willing to abandon the river yet, and said we'd risk it a night or so. He shrugged and got back in the outboard. I shoved the bow free as he jerked the engine to life, and a moment later he was headed north toward town.

I went back to Hazel. "Hope you don't mind, but I think we better move."

She looked at me. "Where?"

"Across the river. We can set up on the land spit between the lake and the mainstream. We'll do it after dark. Dewey hinted we'd be sitting ducks here."

"Ah," she said.

"That's all? No argument?"

"Can't think of any. I don't want to give up the river. And it's hard to believe anybody looking for us would dream we'd just go over by the lake if we were trying to hide out."

"Yeah, well, it may be good only for the night. We'll see."

"But we can eat here, right?"

"Yeah, in case anybody's watching. We'll figure out tomorrow what next."

o reach the new campsite, we had to paddle our loaded canoe upstream about a quarter of a mile, and turn west into the creek that flowed from the lake into the St. Croix. Then we moved south to where a small ridge separated the lake from the river, and located a heavily wooded area near a small, relatively flat spot large enough to use as our hideout. The weather was clear, and I told Hazel we'd sleep in our bedrolls and not raise the tent, which might give us away. It was an awkward and slow process operating in almost total darkness, but we managed. Once she crawled into the sleeping bag, Hazel slept soundly, as far as I could tell. It was late enough that we weren't bothered by mosquitoes.

I kept waking and getting up to look across the silent, dark water. No boats appeared, and no strangers wandered the distant shoreline. The second time I thought I saw a light flash briefly. I was fairly certain it was in the area where we'd camped before, but it was too far to be sure. The only sounds were occasional owl hoots and a brief splashing in the water just south of our ridge. It seemed possible that someone had visited our former campsite, found it deserted, and turned on a flashlight to be sure. After sitting by the water for quite some time without seeing or hearing anything more suspicious, I finally went back to my bedroll.

In the morning I woke and found Hazel fully dressed, sipping coffee by the fire, and gazing back toward the island we had deserted. When she spotted my movement she came over and crouched beside me. "Did you get any sleep before dawn?" she asked.

"Some."

"I must have heard you get up at least three times—you didn't have the trots?"

"Nope. Just checking around. You haven't seen anything since you got up?"

"I watched a muskrat going from his hole by an undercut tree to a patch of brush on the south, where he cut leafy twigs and carried them back home. He's such a primitive-looking thing, all humped and long-tailed, and he lumps along like an arthritic old man. When I walked down to the creek we came in on, I saw a little red squirrel swimming across it, carrying his tail high out of the water so it made a double arch, like a miniature sea monster."

"But no people or boaters?"

"Boaters aren't people?"

"Okay, no hikers or canoeists."

"None. Now what'll we do?"

"Well, I don't like it, but figure we'd better move back to town. We're too easy marks here in the brush."

"So you saw something suspicious last night, huh?"

I told her about the light. She sighed and suggested goosing up the bonfire, which had died down since she made coffee. Then she'd whip up pancakes and bacon.

After eating, we cleaned up, closed camp, loaded the canoe, and started paddling upstream, keeping close to shore on the Minnesota side. The water was glassy smooth, the sky solid blue. A flock of black crows flapped over the water, exchanging squawks that sounded critical of invading canoers. It all seemed so fine I began hating the bastard or bastards who had pitched the body into our lives.

We located a washout spot under the bridge, pulled ashore, and after a quick look-around, climbed a narrow path up to the road and hiked the couple blocks into town. We had moved only a few steps beyond the café when Dewey popped out and caught up. He said he was glad we survived the night, and he looked like he really meant it. Hazel rewarded him with her smile and said she was too.

Nothing new had happened, he told us, and asked what we were planning to do.

"Find a place to stay a couple nights. Any suggestions?"

He was more than glad to help out, and took us to a fairly new local motel on the edge of town that had cabins not much bigger than a country school outhouse. They had a vacancy and were happy to have us move in.

Dewey volunteered his services, drove us back to the bridge, helped haul our personal baggage up to the car, then returned us to the motel and said he knew the people we rented our canoe from—if I wanted, he'd make arrangements to get them to pick it up. He would also get them to store the camping equipment. He promised they wouldn't soak us anything for the storage if we finished our trip later.

Our cabin wasn't a hell of a lot bigger than the tent but was considerably easier to get in and out of, and there were handy his-and-hers privies at the end of the line. Hazel, who rarely complained about anything, said it was sad that while getting up in the morning would be lots easier when you rolled out of a real bed, it was disappointing to look around outside and see nothing but that scruffy yard and forlorn street in view. She was afraid she'd been permanently spoiled by mornings of rising to admire the shining river reflecting blue sky, and the green hills beyond, when she crawled from the tent.

I told her she should just be happy she had a fine-looking man to gaze on. That led to a brief tussle, which ended up on the bed, and we made up for not having shared a sleeping bag the night before.

After making love, we talked. We'd not done that before. It had always been as though once we'd done it, everything was taken care of, and it'd be pointless to gab. But this time the act itself had seemed more like a period of escape, and not the whole point of going to bed. "I keep seeing you grabbing that bloody mess, wondering if you'll really escape getting killed," she told me. "I was even mad that you'd risk this life that's all-important to me for a stranger. I've been feeling guilty ever since, but still, what I thought makes sense. How could you?"

"I never figured on getting killed. There wasn't time to think. If I had, I'd probably have said the hell with it, and hauled you back to the tent for another round."

"And now you want to find out who did it and why. So what are we going to do next?"

"Find friends of Kat, or people who know the family, and wait to see if the body gets a name."

We went to see the sheriff, but he wasn't around, and Dewey didn't have anything new to offer. Nothing developed until Hazel and I were having a late lunch in Klinkhammer's Café at one-thirty. We were just finishing up when a tall, bony young guy walked over from a table nearby and said, "You're Carl Wilcox."

I said I knew that.

"I'm Barry Bacon, Kat's brother."

"Fine, this is Hazel, my wife. Pull over a chair."

His face resembled his sister's, but on a broader scale, especially in the jaw. His hair was deep brown, matching his eyes, and I guessed he was about four years older than Kat. He lounged in the chair, his long legs stretched out straight and knobby hands folded in his lap. He wore a gingham shirt with the sleeves rolled high, exposing surprisingly powerful arms for a man so slender.

"Nobody told us she had a brother," said Hazel.

"Well, you sure wouldn't've heard about me if you just talked with Grandpappy Cole. I turned him down when he asked me to move in with him, after our folks died in their accident, and he took it very personally. You could say I've been disowned by my grandpa. Hell, he always liked Kat better from when she was born. She and I never had any big problems between us—didn't get together much after the accident. But I've kept track of guys Kat's been cozy with, and Dewey got this notion maybe it'd do some good if I talked with you. He and I went to school together and always got along. He told me about you."

I decided it might be just as wise not to ask any questions about that. "So what were you supposed to tell me?"

"Well, a little about what I know of Kat and this band she's involved with."

"Band? What band?"

"The dance band she's been the canary for this past year. Since she started school in Minneapolis. They were in Indeville playing a dance Saturday night."

"So maybe the guy who went over the cliff was there?"

"Could be. I've met all the characters in that bunch, and figure every one of them has been after her from the start. Kat's a girl who can lead guys around by the short hairs, and at the same time she never let any of them really move in, you know?"

"Has she told you that?" asked Hazel.

"She didn't have to, I know how she operates. She gets a big kick out of vamping every guy she knows. She's never let any joker get too far, has been holding them off since she was eleven or so."

"But to keep them hot, she has to give them a certain amount of encouragement, doesn't she?"

"Oh, hell yes. She's always been a great one for smooching and squeezing. Loves all that stuff. But at the same time, Kat's always been smart enough to know she gets more attention when she doesn't let any guy go all the way or get the notion he's her only one."

"Did Dewey show you the dead man?" I asked.

He had straightened up some while answering Hazel's questions. Now he settled back again. "Oh, sure. It was a waste of time. The way the face was smashed up, I wouldn't have known him if he was my twin brother—which I haven't got."

"Could it have been somebody else from the band?"

"It's hard to figure how. I understand they'd all gone back home, to the Twin Cities and places in Wisconsin, like Menomonie."

"You got any notions about why this guy would've been out back of your grandparents' place?"

He shrugged. "Maybe a drunk had to take a leak. Or he was looking for some other neighbor woman. The Bacon place isn't the only house out that way."

"You got some woman around there in mind?"

He looked very doubtful as he shrugged. "I'm just saying there are lots of other possibilities. The local cops want to stick with guys from the band because they're like foreigners. They sure as hell wouldn't ever figure anybody'd get killed by Grandpa Cole or Grandma Katarina."

I granted that was easy to buy.

"Has the band played often around here?" asked Hazel.

"It's more like a few times. Mostly they've been playing in the Twin Cities and around the university there, where they all go to school whenever they can get around to it."

"You remember anything special Kat told you about any of the guys in the band and how they got together?"

"Well, I know that through the school year they were all staying in the same boardinghouse in Minneapolis, right near the U campus. They each had a room of their own and got together about every night to rehearse and plan jobs."

"What can you tell us about the guys?"

"Most of them were sophomores, like her, except the leader, a guy called Tipsy, which I suspect means he's a boozer. I think he's maybe a junior. Plays a great horn and has a way with dance hall owners, according to Kat. Then there's a piano player. A real quiet guy. There's a big dude, Chris Somebody, plays tenor sax. I forget the rest."

"The guy who died wasn't big. Who were the short guys in the band?"

"Hell, I don't know. I guess there were at least two shorties. Now I think of it, there's a guy called Dutch. Can't remember what he does."

"Who's she been involved with around town?" I asked.

"Nobody lately. Used to date Alan Ackroyd in high school. Now he's at the University of Wisconsin. He had a real case on Kat—I heard Alan's father broke that up. Alan wanted to go to the U of Minnesota with the Kat, and his old man put both feet down—right on his neck."

"She have any girlfriends around town?"

"She used to, but now there's nobody real close that I know of."

"Can you think of any reason your sister wouldn't want to name the dead man, even if she knew him?"

"Sure. She couldn't just let herself believe anybody she knows could get killed like that. Kat's a girl who mostly believes what she wants to. Like she's always tried to tell me old Grandpa Cole doesn't really hate me, it's just that he got all shook up because I didn't want to live with them. Felt rejected, she says."

"He told us when he saw Kat nowadays, it was mostly by accident, like in a soda joint or the café. He admitted he got invited to his grandparents' place each Thanksgiving and Christmas, and sometimes he and Kat managed to gab a little."

"You happen to know anything about a guy from around here named Nate Pryke?" I asked.

"Yeah," he admitted, making it sound like a reluctant confession.

"What's your notion of how he died?"

"Well, from what I hear, it wasn't any big surprise. The guy hated farming, wasn't that much involved with his wife. Hell, he was just a lush with nothing going for him but a rich grandpa. It just figures he decided the hell with it all."

"Where'd you hear about him?"

"Oh, hell, there was always lots of gab about him at school because one of the girls there dropped out and married him. You can figure the kind of talk that raised around here. Greatest thing that's happened for the old maids in town."

"Had he been in their school?"

"Hell no, he was lots older. Nobody knows for sure how they met. One story goes she went to New York and met him there, the other is they met at a dance somewhere around here, when she got drunk her first time. A few even claim she wound up getting pregnant so they had to get married. Some figure Pryke wasn't even the guy that knocked her up. All anybody really knows is, the baby never got born. Maybe she had an abortion."

After that report, Barry suddenly seemed to lose interest in the whole business and left us. As he went out the front door, Hazel shook her head. "I think he's lots closer to his sister than he lets on."

"What gives you that idea?"

"Well, the fact he came around, for one thing. And if he's not the loving big brother, how come he paid so much attention to what guys she got involved with, and remembers details about them? He tries to be real offhand about it all, but he can't quite pull it off. I think he wants to be her protector."

"Yeah, if it doesn't put him out too much."

She grinned. "You won't accept him because you like Cole Bacon, and the old man has rejected him. I'd think, considering your relationship with your father, your sympathies would all be with the grandson."

"I've never believed in being consistent. You ever hear the line, 'A foolish consistency is the hobgoblin of little minds'?"

"That's cute, but I don't think it has any bearing on the subject at hand. How come a hobo cowboy like you comes up with lines like that?

"I read a book once, and listen a lot. Let's go around to the sheriff's office."

We found Deputy Dewey sitting in the sheriff's swivel chair. He said the man had gone to have a conference with the mayor.

"Whose idea was that?" I asked.

He gave me an innocent smile and said that every once in a while the sheriff got ideas of his own. Then he asked if Barry had looked me up.

"Yeah. He said you gave him the notion."

"Well, I sort of strong-armed him into it. He give you any ideas?"

"He made it plain he wasn't nuts about his sister's boyfriends. You know any of them?"

"Just Alan, the local boy. None of this band crowd she found at the U. Alan's been in Madison but will be home tonight. How about I take you around to meet him?"

"Does the sheriff know you're doing this?"

"Trying to work with you? Yeah. It seemed like a good idea to me, and while he's not nuts about it, he hasn't said no. Yet. This business may be why he's visiting with the mayor." He grinned at me. "We haven't had a lot of killings around here. It's taking Ernie some time to get into it."

"Ernie—that's Sheriff Steiger's first name?"

"Short for Ernest. Which he is."

"We going around to Alan's home?"

"Well, actually, it might be best to meet him at the beer parlor. He wouldn't like for his dad to know somebody wanted to talk to him about his old true love. That's kind of a sore spot in the family history."

It was about eight in the evening when Hazel and I drifted around to the beer parlor. It was small and smoky with a bar along the entire north wall, and small tables through the center with a row of booths on the south side. There were about a dozen guys hanging around, and they gave Hazel a lot of attention. One guy whistled low. She wasn't bothered. Dewey was in a booth near the back, with a cup of coffee at his elbow. Alan Ackroyd wasn't visible to us until we came near, and he immediately stood up and greeted Hazel while Dewey made introductions. He moved over next to Dewey and let us sit side by side across from them.

Alan had a broad face with a square chin, a high forehead, and more hair than any man needs. He barely gave me a greeting glance; all of his focus was on Hazel. I didn't blame him—in his place, I'd have reacted in the same way. He wanted to know how she liked Wisconsin and apologized for our exposure to murder, as though he took full responsibility for his hometown's lost reputation for purity. She let him know sweetly that she didn't figure it was his fault.

"So," she said after that had been covered, "what do you know about Kat's friends at Minnesota U?"

"Not a lot. Met the gang one night in early June. I was dating Priscilla Peterson, who was in senior high with Kat and me. She's an old friend of Kat's and goes to school with her at Minnesota, so she knows all of her friends there. After school was out and they were both back here, this carload of characters came around, and Kat invited us to join the mob and hit a dance in Stillwater. So we did. Pris had told me a little about these guys, said they were a wild bunch and they called themselves the Kat Klan Fraternity."

"Know any of their names?" I asked.

"Well, there's a guy named Tobler, called Tippy or something, he's the bandleader, and a character they call Link, probably the missing one—"

"Link? He's not one of the guys we've heard mentioned. What's he like?"

"Well, he's not very tall, plays a hell of a trombone, and drinks a lot. He's gaga for the girls but hasn't got a real line, you know? Always trying for more than he can get. He's not bad-looking, exactly, but nothing special, and he tries too hard to make up for it by a lot of talk. At his best he's pretty funny, but he's not up to it all that often."

"You met all these guys the night you mentioned?"

"Yeah, like I said, we all drove over to Stillwater for a dance one Saturday night a while back. They were so wild and noisy I thought we'd get thrown out, but it never quite came to that."

"When did you break up with Kat?"

"Oh hell, I gave her up my last year in high school. She was too much for any one guy."

"Are you saying she'd take anybody on?"

"No, no, nothing like that. It's just that she's always getting the big rush. Back at high school dances guys would line up to get a turn with her, and she just got a big kick out of it and encouraged them. But she's never dated just anybody, or let the few that get close do more than maybe some heavy petting. She's too smart to let any joker go too far. I finally gave her up because there were just always too many guys panting after her, and she enjoyed all that too much."

"Were you at the dance last Saturday night?"

"No, but I heard about it. Drew a darned good crowd. Priscilla and I went to a movie instead."

"Could we get together with Priscilla?" asked Hazel.

"Maybe—I can give her a call—"

"Ask her to join us."

When Alan was gone, Dewey leaned toward me. "Who told you about the band business?"

"Her brother, Barry. He said it was your idea he come around."

He nodded and sat back, smiling.

Alan returned in a few moments and said if we wanted to see Priscilla, we'd have to go over to her place. I gathered either she or her parents didn't approve of beer joints. She was sitting on a wicker chair on a broad porch as we approached, and stood as we climbed the three steps. Her nose was turned up, her chin round, and she had classroom eyes, pale blue, wide open, and a bit too wise. She paid little attention to Dewey, being already familiar with him, but her examination of Hazel and me was more than thorough. For a change, I got the most attention.

Priscilla was not a young woman who gave any clues about her impressions. She smiled formally and did not offer a hand but welcomed us politely, waved us toward the wicker couch against the wall under the front windows, and went back to her seat in the chair near the railing on the east side of the porch. Alan, Hazel, and I took the couch; Dewey rested his fanny on the handiest railing.

Priscilla said she understood we had been canoeing on the St. Croix and asked how we liked it. Hazel assured her it was beautiful, just as wonderful as she remembered when she canoed on it as a teenager.

"Isn't it strange," said Priscilla, "that of all the people who've canoed on that river, a man with experience in investigating murders would be the one handy when the first murder any of us have ever known happened right near town. Would you call that serendipity?"

"I might," said Hazel. "I'm not sure the local sheriff sees it that way."

"How about his deputy?" Priscilla's blue eyes nailed Dewey.

"Oh," he said, waving his hand, "I'd say you hit it right on the nose—or something."

He didn't know any more about what serendipity meant than I did.

I asked Priscilla if she'd seen the body of the murdered man. She said no.

"Would you be willing to take a look?"

"No, thanks. I don't see any use in it."

"It seems pretty likely to me that the murdered man was one of the guys in the band Kat Bacon sings with. How well do you know them? Would you likely recognize one of them?"

"I never really got to know any of them personally. Always the outsider. From what Kat told me, it doesn't seem likely anyone would recognize what was left after the fall. And if Kat isn't able to identify him, I certainly couldn't."

"Did any of the band guys ever come around to her home?"

"Oh, sure, at least a couple times Kat told me about. She said Cole let them know he thought they were nitwits blowing their brains out through horns. They took that well, kidded him back, and all the while treated Kat like she was a movie star. She just loved it and made up to every one of them. She loves the whole gang. You know they all live in the same apartment building, right on the edge of the campus in Minneapolis? They don't belong to any Greek fraternity—they're all very scornful of those who do. They get jobs at private parties, even play in some of the frat houses. Each time they get a job they pile into Tipsy's station wagon with all their instruments carried in a box on the roof. It holds all six of them easily. They call it their riot wagon."

"Did they come together in it for the Saturday dance?"

"No, I think there were two or three cars—the three from the Twin Cities in one, and the others in their own."

"Any of them do any other work?" I asked.

"Oh, I think Watson waited tables at a campus café. As far as I remember, Link didn't do much but play his horn, drink a lot, and moon over women. I guess Tipsy has had some kind of job in the cities. I seem to remember hearing his father set it up for him."

"And maybe supplied the station wagon?"

"It's certainly possible. They get along very well with each other."

"Who else was in the Kat Klan?"

"Well, there was a blond fellow named Haar. I can't remember his real first name, but Tipsy called him Dutch. He was about Link's size, only a little broader. There were two others, both fairly tall. One they call 'Skinny.' Then there's Chris Christenson, who has a good build and dresses very smartly, but that's all I can remember. Except they both have dark hair. Come to think of it, I heard the skinny one, Engen, was from Menomonie."

Alan spoke up again. "I heard Tipsy say the one they call Chris is either the son of a doctor or was planning to go to med school."

"Kat told me his father was a doctor, that's all I know," said Priscilla.

I got the feeling she wanted to seem uninterested in the whole gang. They offended her, probably because they ignored her.

Eventually Hazel and I left with Dewey, and he suggested we swing around to the sheriff's office and see if the man had come back.

A half a block from city hall we met the sheriff walking with a small, gray-haired man in a dark striped suit, who he introduced as Mayor Goodwin. The mayor had bushy gray eyebrows above rimless glasses, narrow nostrils, a wide smiling mouth, and a dimpled chin. He didn't quite ooze charm, but you did get a sense that for him, there was always an election coming up, and he wasn't about to lose a vote by hiding his loving nature. He told us, while looking us over carefully in turn, how deeply he regretted the shocking experience we'd been exposed to, but how grateful he was that we were so willing to help discover what made it all happen. "I understand," he said, looking at me, "that you've had broad experience in murder detection, even solved several cases. Is that right?"

I allowed there'd been a few.

"Well, I've talked to some fine citizens who're willing to raise a reasonable stake to offer as a reward for anyone able to solve this business. Deputy Dewey tells me you might be helpful. I believe we could arrange for an advance to cover your expenses of staying in town, and if you manage to clear up this mess, we would see to it that you were rewarded for your services. Does this interest you?"

"It fascinates us," said Hazel.

The mayor grinned at her, then shook hands all around and said that was settled. He suggested we work out with the sheriff what immediate compensation we needed, and he'd provide us with a check tomorrow. Now he was going home, and he felt he might sleep better knowing we were on the job.

The sheriff was suffering through all of this, but he kept his mouth shut, obviously feeling obligated to go along with the mayor, whatever it cost him personally. Before parting with the sheriff, I mentioned that Barry Bacon, Kat's brother, had said Link owned a fairly new Olds, and asked if a stray car like that had been noticed around the Bacon farm, or anywhere in town. He said no, but grudgingly promised to have his men look around for one.

As we headed for our motel, Hazel asked me if I thought I'd sleep as well as the mayor hoped to.

"With your help, like a log. But I think the sheriff will toss some."

Hazel shook her head. "I almost feel sorry for him. You really must try to be kind to him."

"I'll work on it."

either one of us slept worth a dandelion seed. After a bit of loving we went over what to do next, and finally decided we had to get full names and addresses for as many of the Kat Klan as Kat could produce. Eventually we drifted off, but we got up early and after breakfast hiked over to the Bacons' home.

Kat answered our knock and let us in as if we had been invited. Cole and Mrs. Bacon were in the kitchen, where their granddaughter led us, and asked us to sit down with them and have some coffee. They had just finished breakfast.

I explained my deal with the mayor and asked Kat if she could get any of her friends to come and try identifying the body. She made it plain she didn't care for the idea at first, but when her grandmother suggested it might turn into a party, Kat got interested and said she'd call the ones living in Wisconsin, and even if the party ended up as something of a wake, it would be worth a try. She asked her grandfather if it'd be okay to make the calls. He said yes, but it was plain he didn't like any part of the whole business, and his tone was grudging. Kat beamed at him, then invited me to stay in the kitchen and went to the living room, where they had their phone. I heard her crank for the operator and give her a number, but from then on the voice was too low to overhear. Hazel started talking with the grandmother, who let us know she was tickled by her grandniece's involvement with the Klan but had some big doubts about its future. She said it was all too unnatural, even a little spooky, with all these fellows so crazy about one girl. She thought it was bound to break up the band in the long run. Cole kept his silence and the disapproving scowl.

Kat finished up her calls in a surprisingly short time and returned to the kitchen, looking smug. After pouring a cup of coffee she sat down with us.

"Reach everybody?" asked her grandmother.

"Not everybody, but I got Chris and Skinny. They'll be around a little after supper."

I asked for their full names, and she said Chris was Theodore Christenson and Skinny was Orville Engen. Chris lived in Chippewa Falls. His uncle was the foreman of the bottling plant where Chris worked summers his last two years in high school. It was heavy work and had given him the muscles of a weight lifter. Skinny had grown up in Menomonie. His father was an English teacher and directed the school band. Both young men had been willing to come and look at the body.

We left and went to find the sheriff in his office. He said yes, the corpse was still available. He was caught somewhere between defiance and embarrassment when he explained about arrangements made to store it in the local butcher's refrigerated room to keep it preserved long enough for further identification efforts.

I explained to him about the guys Kat knew that might recognize the dead man. When I said they'd be around a bit after supper to take a look, he brightened up, then told me the mayor had arranged for me to use a Model A from the local Ford dealer.

"It's yours as long as you're helping out on this thing. Ed's even got it all gassed up for you. But you got to agree to use it only for the business at hand, you know?"

That sounded fine to me, since it meant I wouldn't have to go back to where we had rented the canoe and get my Model T. We went over to the dealer's and met Ed, who was one of those nonstop talkers. It was plain he had the notion that the loan was more like a trial run, after which I'd naturally buy the car because it was so irresistible and Ed was such a great guy. By the time we drove away from his place I had decided I wouldn't buy from this bastard if he offered to sell me a new Cadillac for a quarter.

It was fun driving the Model A, with its gear-shift clutch and no need for a crank, and a motor that purred like a whopping cat with a chest cold.

We headed for the Bacons' house at the edge of town, pulling off the road into ruts that led up to a gate in a fence running between the road and a pasture. This was near where the guy had gone over the cliff, and I felt like looking around the area again. As we neared the bluffs over the river, we saw brush and the dense green leaves of the small forest that grew everywhere there was earth for roots along the rocky bluffs above the St. Croix. The grass and weeds were too thick to give any real hints of what may have happened before that body had been launched into space, but there were a couple spots where the pasture had been flattened in erratic patterns.

Hazel watched me rubbernecking around and, when I finally gave up, asked what it told me.

"Damn little. I can't see a thing that'd even suggest there was a real fight anywhere around here. No scuffing, no patches of flattened grass you might get in a wrestle. What bothers me is the shot. It sounded like a shotgun to me, but who the hell fired it?"

After eating a good dinner in the café, we went to the car and drove back to the Bacon house, where we spotted a boxy green Chevy coupe parked in the driveway to the garage. Kat answered my knock and again let us in, giving me her warm smile. She had a way of acting as though Hazel and she were old classmates and I was a long-missing friend.

A tall guy was standing near the window. He was rangy, with sloping shoulders and a sinewy neck. His eyebrows were craggy, his nose slightly hooked, and his wide smile showed narrowly gapped white teeth. This, Kat told us, was Theodore "Chris" Christenson. He moved forward, nodded at Hazel, offered me his big, bony hand, and didn't try to mangle my smaller one. The other guy, who'd been sitting on the couch, stood up, bowed to Hazel, and offered me a hand more my size. He was Orville Engen, and it was plain why they called him Skinny. His face was nearly skeletal, his neck lean, and his shoulders sharp. I couldn't help imagining him in a coffin. He had examined Hazel with approving pale blue eyes, but when he took me in, his expression was blank and distant. He spoke in a velvet voice and did not smile.

I asked if they'd been to town to check the body yet. Chris said no, they wanted to stop by and see Kat first.

"Did she tell you what she thought of it?"

"We didn't talk about that," he said in a mildly disapproving tone.

"It'd be pretty natural. You ready to go look now?"

He glanced at Kat, who said they might as well get it over with.

We drove in our separate cars, going to see the sheriff first, who promptly took the two guys over to the butcher shop after copying down their names and addresses and asking a few general questions. The walk-in refrigerator was a small room, made even smaller by the human body laid out on boards over sawhorses.

The sheriff took the guys in, one at a time. Chris went first. There was no question about the identification when he came out. His face was grim, his eyes dull.

"Recognize him?" I asked.

"Yeah. Francis Linklater. We called him Link. Everybody did." He looked for a place to sit down and, finding none, leaned against the butcher's display counter as his buddy Skinny Engen followed the sheriff into the cooler.

"How'd you recognize him?" I asked Chris.

He stirred, as if I'd intruded on a dream, then took a deep breath and straightened up to face me. "The hands are the give-away. He had the stubbiest thumbs I ever saw. You couldn't miss them. I kidded him once, saying they were so short he'd never make it as a hitchhiker. He thought that was very funny."

Engen's face was relatively unexpressive when he came out. The sheriff led us outside and back to his office. The interview didn't take long. Dewey sat near and took notes. Engen backed up Chris's comments on the thumbs, and added that he had particularly noticed the ears—he remembered they had large lobes with a distinct crease. I asked them to tell us about the dance job that last night—how had it gone, whether anything unusual had happened, and what took place once it was over.

Chris said it had gone very well; they drew a good crowd, and Kat was enthusiastically applauded every time she sang. No, he didn't remember anything unusual happening.

"What about the intermission—anybody in particular team up?"

"Well," said Chris, "actually we all went to the restaurant across the street from the hall where Kat had arranged for us to have beers in a back room. We made it a party for her because she'd lined up the job and pulled in this big crowd, and we wanted to show her how much we appreciated it all."

"What was the setup—you all sit around a table or line up at a bar—?"

"No, there was this buffet with stuff to eat and a bartender who served us beer, and we just stood around and talked, mostly. We didn't have much time, you know."

"Did Link try to move in on Kat?"

"Well, no. As a matter of fact, Link brought a girlfriend along. Carmen somebody—"

"Pryke," said Kat. I glanced her way. Her face was expressionless, but the tone was, for her, mighty cool.

"Was that a girl who was in high school with you?" asked Hazel.

"She wasn't in my class." For a second she considered that, then added, "She was a year ahead of me."

"A friend of yours?"

"No. We didn't have any classes together."

"So she was a gate-crasher?"

"Link brought her, so that made her a guest." Her tone was only slightly grudging.

We learned that Link's father was a lawyer in South St. Paul, the home of three major meatpacking plants. All the gang called it Stinkytown, not to be confused with Dinkytown, the shopping area near the center of the University of Minnesota's main campus. Link was a year younger than his friends and had told them a lot about his school days; he'd skipped a grade in his fourth year of school because he was too bright for his class and had a very tough time adjusting to the jump. While most of the class tolerated him, he was unhappy for the first month, and never felt really accepted by his new classmates, who mostly kept him at a distance. But after about a month he was doing fine as a student and getting top grades again. He'd never gone into details about relations with his classmates, but the band partners figured all had not been cozy.

"What happened after the dance?" I asked. "Everybody take off?"

"Just Link. He and Carmen went their way; the rest of us rented a cabin overnight, then on Sunday took a canoe trip on the river."

"I wasn't at the cabin," said Kat. "I slept at home, then went with the guys on the river, riding with Haar and Tipsy, while Watson and Skinny shared with Chris."

"That's right," said Chris. "We paddled a ways downstream, mostly just drifting, had a lunch of hot dogs, and went swimming, sunned, and drank a little beer."

"Was it pretty unusual for Link not to be partying with your gang?" I asked.

"Not especially," said Chris. He made that sound very casual.

I looked at Kat, could guess nothing from her blank face, and looked around at the others. "Why would this guy Link be wandering around here somewhere between three and four in the morning?" I asked. "Had he ever come around your place before?"

"Not alone," she said, speaking very carefully. "He'd just come with the other fellows in the band. You never quite knew what to expect from him. He was never that predictable."

"Somehow," said Hazel, "I get a feeling you people are holding back on us. Was there some rivalry in this bunch about who was closest to Kat?"

Christenson's smile was close to condescending. "Not at all. We were very careful about that kind of thing, because we all knew it could raise hell with the band's future."

"I don't know if you heard," I said, "but the night of the killing, there was a shot fired just a little before Link screamed and went over the cliff. Any of you know if Link owned or ever carried a gun?"

There was no immediate response, but when I looked at Chris, since I figured he had probably been closest to Link, he frowned and said yes, he did remember Link had bought one, but he thought he just kept it in his car. He'd had trouble with a tough guy once who got sore because his date got too interested in Link, so he figured he needed a little backup since he wasn't very big or handy with his mitts.

"You ever see it?"

"Yeah. It was a little .32. A five-cylinder job."

Skinny said he guessed he had heard about the gun but didn't remember ever seeing it.

I asked if they might be able to talk other members of the gang into coming around to help get this murder figured out. Skinny looked doubtfully at Chris, who frowned and said he'd be willing to give it a shot. He knew their telephone numbers and schedules well enough to make connections, but warned that it might take a day or so. Haar and Tipsy, in particular, got around a lot.

The sheriff took the other guys' full names; Phil (Tipsy) Tobler, Jan (Dutch) Haar, and Nolan Watson. I asked how come Watson was the only one without a nickname and Skinny said it was because Tipsy wanted to call him Doc but he wouldn't stand for that, and somehow nobody else ever came up with anything that stuck.

Sheriff Steiger asked the guys if they could give him Linklater's father's address or telephone number. They had no ideas, so he called the long-distance operator, who gave him the number and made the call. Whoever answered said no, the son had not been living at home for some time, and they didn't know where he was. The sheriff asked to speak with Oran Linklater. He was asked to hold, and while waiting he put his hand over the mouthpiece and told us he was going to let him know what had happened to his son, and have him come around for the identification. He asked if the guys knew the license number of Link's car. They didn't. Chris said he thought that it was a Minnesota plate. The sheriff thanked them and said we might as well leave.

The guys went back to the Bacons' for another visit with Kat, and I took Hazel to visit the town mayor. After some discussion, he agreed to cover gas costs for our trip to Minneapolis for talks with the other three band members. He even offered to cover an over nighter if that was necessary.

That evening in the motel room, Hazel and I went over the day, and she generally agreed with my notions of the characters we'd met.

"The best thing for me," she said, "is learning about the band. I could never believe it was Kat alone that held them together. I mean, that many guys just don't stay in the clouds long enough to chase after one unobtainable girl for as long as these seemed to. But what about this Carmen character? Can you imagine Link bringing a woman like that around to the party, and how Kat must have reacted?"

"I don't know. Maybe a guy who's such a whiz as a student has a lot of imagination—figured he might make Kat jealous, trick her into competing."

Hazel shook her head thoughtfully. "I'm beginning to wonder if there wasn't something going on inside this band bunch. But nothing we've heard so far makes it seem like any of them would've had it in for Link. Certainly not enough for them to pitch him over the cliff."

We kicked the whole business around some more but eventually went to sleep without anything more than a little smooching because her period had begun.

"Now I know why they call it the curse," I said.

"The hell you do," she told me.

I called the Minneapolis police department Thursday morning and reached Sergeant Logan, who had helped me a couple years back.

"What kind of trouble you in now?" he asked.

"It's pretty serious. I'm on my honeymoon in Indeville, Wisconsin."

"Wha-at?"

"You heard me."

"Yeah, but I can't believe it. Why call me? You sure as hell don't need any help in handling a woman."

"We got a special problem. Somebody dropped a body in our laps when we were camping on an island a couple miles from here, and it's kind of complicated things. I'll be in town today— could you get loose around chow time after work?"

"This body—did it come from Minneapolis?"

"Not that morning—but originally it came from South St. Paul. Some of this guy's buddies are your neighbors. I'm coming around to look them up, and I figured it might help if you could let me know whether they had any kind of a police record."

I gave him the names Tobler, Watson, and Haar, explaining that the latter was from South St. Paul, but the others were Minneapolitans.

"How about the guy killed?"

"Francis Linklater, called Link. He's from South St. Paul."

He said he'd have Flynn check them out and asked when I'd show up.

"We'll leave here in about an hour—should get into town early enough to meet you after working hours."

Logan told me nobody could be too sure about his hours, but if we'd show up at Charlie's Café for supper, he'd see us there. He guessed that Flynn would be as eager as he was to see a woman who could nail me down.

After getting the mayor's check for $25 and cashing it at the bank, Hazel and I ate lunch and took off. It was a clear, hot day, and we drove with the windows down and the hot air whipping through the car all the way. She wore a scarf over her head and read Twain's *Life on the Mississippi*. Every once in a while she'd read a paragraph aloud.

I said that on our fiftieth anniversary, we'd take a canoe trip on the Mississippi. The sound that brought was suspiciously close to a snort, but with her being a lady, no doubt I heard that wrong.

The scenery was best when we drove near the St. Croix River. The valley was moderately deep and well wooded; it looked lush and green, in complete contrast with the dried-out South Dakota territory so familiar to me. We finally skirted St. Paul and entered Minneapolis. I paid attention to the map we'd picked up in a Wisconsin gas station and didn't get lost, although the territory we covered seemed strange to me. I'd only traveled areas on the west side of the city during previous trips. We went by the university, crossed the Washington Avenue Bridge, wheeled on in moderate traffic toward downtown, made a left turn near the railroad station, and parked in a lot behind the restaurant. The place looked like a fairly large private home, with its white clapboard siding and shingled roof.

It was almost six when we walked into the dark, cool interior and sighted Flynn talking to a bartender in the first room. A glance around located Logan at a table nearby, and we went over to join him. I thought he looked a little heavier than before, but just more solid, not fat.

Logan took one look at Hazel and got up, smiling like a loving father.

"Well," he said, "we've always known old Carl had a way with the ladies, but I'd never have believed he'd settle for just one. Until now."

"Flattery will get you almost anywhere," Hazel told him, "but Carl's already warned me about you. I mean, what a fine policeman you are."

"I'll bet. Sit down and tell me how come you got trapped into this fix. Maybe we can pin something on him and get you free."

She grinned, accepted the offered chair, and said, "That's not my ambition, at least not so far. How's crime in the big city?"

"Oh, we've about wiped it out. Nothing to worry about since Prohibition ended, except there's so cockeyed many people driving cars all of us may wind up being traffic cops. How come you ask? Is Carl looking for a real job now he's hitched?"

Flynn abandoned his bartender and joined us, cutting off whatever response Hazel had in mind as he took her in with an eager gleam in his eye. After introductions and a bit more chatter, Logan got down to cases. "We don't have zip on your boy Nolan Watson, and the record's clear on Philip Tobler. We do just happen to have a few things on Tobler's old man. He's been running a pawnshop downtown for years. There've been rumors that he deals in stolen goods, but so far we've never been able to nail him."

"Did you come up with anything on the South St. Paul guy, Haar?" I asked.

"Oh, sure. He'd been in big trouble—was with a gang that did some vandalizing one Halloween. Soaping windows or something awful like that, when he was about eleven or twelve. From all we've got, it doesn't look much like your boys are exactly a tough bunch."

"Or maybe they've just been smart."

"Maybe. How about we get down to this guy that took the header into your camp?"

"Actually, he didn't quite make it to our camp. We were pretty well down below the railroad track he smacked at about four in the morning."

I gave him the details, and he shook his head and looked at Flynn. "Can you figure any other guy you've ever met who'd go charging into a murder case while on his honeymoon?"

"Absolutely, positively none," said Flynn.

When they were through being cute, Logan asked about the nearest neighbors to the murder scene, and I told him about the Bacon family. Flynn leaned closer to the table.

"You say the daughter's name was Katarina Bacon?"

I nodded. Flynn turned to Logan. "You remember a call about an attempted rape near the U? Wasn't that the girl's name?"

"Yeah—it was the kind of name sticks with you. Now let's see, what was the name of the guy she accused?"

Flynn grinned at me. "It was Linklater. Nicknamed Link. The other guy you asked about."

"What came of the case?"

"Well, sir, it was pretty interesting. She called us the morning after. When we gave her a hard time about not reporting the case the night it happened, she got all flustered, then mad, and said if we were going to be like that, she'd drop the charges. And she did."

I considered that some, then asked if he'd got any dope on Linklater's old man.

He grinned at me. "For what it's worth, we know his old man's a lawyer, named Oran. And on a couple occasions he's been old Tobler's mouthpiece."

"Like what occasions?"

"When we tried to nail him for dealing in stolen goods."

"Was the lawyer pretty good?"

"He was plenty good enough to keep us from nailing the bastard."

fter a few calls I found a Haar number. The woman who
answered said yes, her son Jan was home, and called him to
the phone. He was politely suspicious at first, but also
curious, and it didn't take much persuading to convince him he
should let us come around.

It was a warm and breezy evening. We found the house with
no trouble, parked in front, and walked up to the sloping porch,
where a stocky young man was sitting on a porch swing. He got
up to meet us, and like every other guy we met, turned friendly
as a spaniel pup the minute he piped Hazel's brown eyes and
greeting smile. His responding grin half closed his pale blue eyes
and showed small white teeth and deep dimples. He was about
my height but outweighed me by a good twenty pounds, without
looking fat. Hazel and I sat in battered wicker chairs, while he
went back to the swing.

Yes, he'd heard what had happened in Wisconsin and was
sorry about it, and of course he was shocked. He had no idea why
Link would be around the Bacons' home and couldn't imagine
he had been visiting them.

"Why not?" I asked.

"Well, it was just that none of us tried to move in alone. We were more like a goofy fraternity. And she'd made it real plain to us that her grandpa wasn't nuts about the band and would raise hell if one of us came around alone, trying to hustle her."

"What about when Kat called the police and accused Linklater of attempted rape?"

He gave me a sheepish grin, raised both hands as if in surrender, and shook his head sorrowfully. "She just lost her temper because he got a little carried away when he walked her home that night. It was nothing serious. She dropped the charge."

"When was this?"

"Just before the Easter break."

"Where'd it happen?"

"In her apartment. It didn't amount to anything."

Hazel and I sat in silence for a few seconds, watching him. He squirmed a little.

"Who in your crowd was the number-one guy for Kat?" I asked.

He turned very serious. "Kat never played any favorites. She was smart enough to be real careful she didn't do anything that'd split up the Klan."

"Somewhere along the line, I got the notion Tipsy was her big moment."

"Well, you probably got that from Tipsy. He likes to believe he's top dog anywhere. That doesn't mean he's right."

"I hear your gang partied once with an old high school boyfriend of hers, Alan Ackroyd. What'd you think of him?"

"I didn't really get to know him. Seemed okay. Brought a girlfriend of his own."

"Priscilla Peterson."

Haar smiled.

"Why does that make you smile?" asked Hazel.

"Well, nobody was fooled into thinking Alan took her seriously. She wasn't in the same class with Kat when it comes to looks. He brought her along because she'd been an old pal of Kat's, and he knew she'd appreciate it. His real interest was in Kat, just like everybody else's."

"Didn't you see Priscilla around the U in Minneapolis?"

"Not much. I don't think she was ever really comfortable with us. She didn't fit and knew it. Her old man is loaded with dough, which makes her real big with Kat's grandpa, and I think Kat sort of felt obligated to be her chum and make the old man happy, since he was really against all the band business. When she and Kat got together, it was just the two of them."

"I've got some trouble with this whole business," I said. "Are you telling me that six guys ran around at the heels of Kat, like a dog pack, and nobody ever made out?"

"I'm telling you we all went for her. She liked us, and it was kind of a club. What's wrong with that? You think we were all sleeping with her?"

"It'd take a big bed."

He decided that was funny and laughed.

"How often was she alone with any of you guys?" I asked.

"Well, it was nearly never. I mean, we all lived in the same apartment building, so nobody had to go pick her up when we were doing a job or going out to party. We just took off all together in Tipsy's crate. Once in a while one of us would walk her home when we'd been out someplace reasonably close by on campus and she wanted to leave early. I don't think she ever dated anybody outside the Klan. Hell, she didn't have any time. We used to practice almost every night for at least a while there. She didn't have time to run around, and neither did we. She lunched with Priscilla sometimes, and for all I know, maybe a guy or two joined them."

"So how come Link made his pass?"

"Well, we'd done a dance that pulled a good crowd, and all of us were feeling really good about it and had more drinks than usual afterward. Kat wasn't much into that and decided she wanted to go home. Link jumped right in and offered to take her, and she said okay. I guess Link had already been nipping between breaks, and when he got her back to the apartment he was pretty high and got a little carried away when she made the mistake of inviting him in for a few minutes. It gave him big ideas, and he just got too pushy."

"How'd you guys take that?"

"Oh, we were all real mad at first, but then Kat told us to forget it all, and we were kind of relieved to go along. Link was a hell of a good man on the slip horn and not a real bully.

"We heard Link had a pretty fancy car for a fellow not earning big money," said Hazel. "Are his parents rich?"

"They can afford to eat regularly, I guess. I don't really know."

"Did he seem to have more money than the other guys?"

"He didn't exactly throw it around. I don't know."

"You didn't really know him well at all, did you?"

"Well, we only grew up in the same town together, we weren't like family."

"How'd you get to Wisconsin for the last band job?"

"I rode with Tobler in his crate."

When I asked how he got back, he said it was the same way. I asked if he knew whether Link owned a gun. He admitted he'd heard of it, but not seen it. Finally I asked who'd told him about Link's death. He said Kat had telephoned to tell him.

We thanked him for his time, said good-bye, and headed back to our hotel, both convinced he'd been holding something back. We agreed that he had not liked Link, and were surprised he tried to make us think he was all right.

"Wouldn't you think he'd unload a little?" Hazel asked as we drove away.

"Nah, he's the kind of guy who just doesn't knock anybody he's been close to one way or another. Matter of honor. What we need is a gossiper, a knocker in the crowd. They can't all be sweethearts."

aar gave us an address for his two friends, Tipsy Tobler and Nolan Watson. They were still living in the apartment house near the main campus a block off of University Avenue, which had been the headquarters of the group through the previous school year. We wheeled around, located the address, and parked in front, close to trolley tracks. The place looked like a once-upon-a-time mansion gone to seed, with a large porch, sturdy columns linked by a rusting chain, and a wide front walk that was cracked and crumbling.

A young couple sat in folding chairs on the left side. There was no light on the porch. They had been tilting toward each other when we approached and straightened up the moment they heard us.

I asked if this was where Phil Tobler and Nolan Watson lived.

The girl said she thought there was a Tobler on the second floor. "You can check the mailboxes inside there."

I thanked her, and we went into the front hall, which was wide, with a broad staircase upward on the right and a dim bare bulb glowing in a fixture overhead.

The numbers on the mailboxes ran from 1 to 12. Tobler was under 11. There was no Watson listed. We climbed the creaking stairs and followed a meandering hallway with a series of threadbare carpets to a door on the right side. The door had a curtained window in the upper half. No light came from inside.

I knocked and got no answer. A second try brought a response from the door behind us. "If you're looking for Tipsy, you're too early," said a squeaky voice.

We turned to see a skinny guy in baggy slacks and a blue shirt, grinning at us from a doorway across the hall. He looked like an unsuccessful panhandler.

"When's the best time to find him home?" I asked.

"Probably between two A.M. and two P.M. But he ain't awful sociable except on weekends."

"What's he do?"

"He blows a helluva horn, that's all I know."

"You know a guy named Nolan Watson?"

"Sure. The caretaker. He's in the basement."

"I didn't see him listed on the postal boxes."

"Well, the basement hasn't got a number, and old Watson's the shy type—he never got around to putting his own name up. Mailman goes down and shoves his stuff in the door slot."

I thanked him, and we went down to the basement. There was a light under the door, and my knock brought a prompt "Yeah." A second later the door opened.

The young man facing us was a little over my height, with sandy-colored curly hair, a snub nose, blue eyes, and a firm chin.

I introduced Hazel, whose greeting smile brought his eyes to bright life, and told him my name. His eyes snapped back to me and opened a fraction wider.

"Yes?" he said.

"Like to talk with you a few minutes."

He struck me as a man who would normally ask why, but instead he just nodded, backed up a step to admit us, and moved over to an easy chair in the corner of the broad room. There was an old upright piano against the eastern wall, with the ivory missing from a couple keys. Near the piano was a set of drums.

"I've got the feeling you've heard my name," I said when we were seated.

"That's right. Talked with Dutch. He said you'd probably be around. About what happened to Link."

"What do you think of what happened?"

He shook his head, frowning. "I can't really believe it. Link just wasn't a guy you'd expect anything violent would happen to."

"Really? From everything we've been hearing, I'd guess he was ripe for trouble a good share of the time—especially when he was drunk."

He shook his head slowly, but frowned and finally shrugged.

"I don't know. In some ways he was a hard guy to figure. Absolutely the best natural horn man I ever met, but it never made him anything like cocky. He was bothered about being ordinary looking and having trouble making out with girls. It always seemed weird to me because, you come right down to it, he was smarter than most of us, and he knew it, and I got the feeling he felt he shouldn't have to prove anything and the girls should just get in line. And sometimes he'd sulk around. But I can't imagine him jumping off a cliff, or making somebody mad enough to kill him. Is it a positive ID?"

"You better believe it. Chris and Skinny both recognized him on sight, even with his face all smashed in."

"How about Kat?"

"She wasn't sure. I don't think she could make herself look him over too closely."

Watson smiled. "Yeah, Kat generally believes just what she wants to. That can be pretty handy."

"How'd you guys come together?"

"Well, for one thing we've all lived here at Kellerman's ever since school started last fall. I was the second one after Haar. Then Tipsy came around, and in pretty short order we found out all of us had been in high school bands, and I guess you could say none of us was unhappy about being away from home and getting around with guys who thought pretty much the way we did, liked a little drinking and a lot of jawing. When Kat heard us playing down here one night, she knocked and asked did we need a singer, and hell, who wouldn't have given her a chance? We'd probably have taken her on without even hearing her sing, but Tipsy asked her to, and she was terrific. We all fell for her, bang! It was really exciting."

"Did she ever go all the way with any of you guys?"

"Oh, hell no, she's way too smart for that. She'd know it'd make anybody left out feel jealous as hell, and it'd cause all kinds of problems. I'll tell you something, Kat's not just a knockout with talent, she's always figuring the angles and percentages. That gal wants to go to the top."

"So how come she let Link into her room when she knew he was drunk and horny?"

"Well, the smartest of us make mistakes, right? I figure she thought he was too savvy to think she'd ever stand for it. Hell, I'd have thought so too, because he's no dummy. But you get a guy with his talent on the horn and enough to drink, he can all of a sudden get the big head, and there's no telling what the hell he'll do. The one thing Kat didn't have figured right was how much she gave guys ideas. She loved getting a man up, but she didn't realize how nuts a guy can get, you know?" He glanced at Hazel with an apologetic expression. She looked innocent. It was enough to make me look at her twice.

I turned back to Watson. "So you're the caretaker here?"

"Yeah. Mrs. Kellerman owns the joint. I've been on the job a year and a half. She knew my ma and hired me by phone. Believe it or not, I've never seen her. I get free rent and a little check that comes on the first by mail. Every now and again she gives me a call to see if I need anything."

"You get any vacations?"

"Well, I can't afford a trip to Florida, so I don't need much time off."

"Is Tobler the only one of the gang still living here besides you?"

"That's right."

"How does he pay his way through school?"

"He sure didn't make it blowing a horn. His old man takes care of his expenses through the school year. This summer he wangled a job for Tipsy, selling clothes downtown at a men's store. Juster's. Actually I figure he's working there for the stuff he can buy at a discount and the people he gets to talk with. He's a born pitch artist and clotheshorse."

"I gather the band practices here," said Hazel, looking around.

"Sure. It's the biggest apartment, and it has its own refrigerator. Most of the tenants have to share a hall icebox. I like having the guys practice in my rooms, because I figure it's best for the other tenants. Besides," he said with a broad grin, "it wouldn't have been easy for me to carry the piano up to anybody else's room."

"Where'd you get the piano?"

He looked over at it and smiled. "My mom gave it to me. Dad bought it for her when they were first married, and she taught me to play it soon as I was big enough to reach the keys. She got arthritis in her hands and had to quit playing, so when I came here, she just sent it with me."

"Is Tipsy the leader of the band?"

"You got it."

"Weren't any of you guys involved with other chicks?"

"Oh sure, we all fooled around some. But nobody any of us met seemed like much with Kat around. Girls we dated couldn't compete with her, and got wise to that in a hurry."

I asked where Tipsy might be right now, and he said that was hard to say. He often stayed out late. When Hazel and I decided to leave, Watson went with us up to the front door. The couple had abandoned the porch, and as we were saying good-bye to Watson, a station wagon swung into the drive beside the house and drove toward the back parking area. "You're in luck," said Watson. "That's Tipsy."

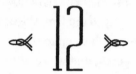

W atson led us around toward the back door, and we intercepted the young man as he headed for the entrance on the east side, toward the south end of the apartments.

Watson introduced us. The light above the door showed a guy just a shade over six feet tall, with furry eyebrows, a wide mouth, and a sharp-edged chin. His hair was light brown and looked as if it had been marcelled. He glanced at me and examined Hazel, smiling so his even teeth gleamed. When Watson told him what we were after, the smile faded, and he managed to look thoughtful. He gave me the feeling that any expression he got except the smile had to be produced deliberately, and he worked at it.

Tipsy invited us up to his room and included Watson, who shook his head, saying he had things to do.

We went up the stairs and entered Tipsy's apartment. The first room was a large kitchen with garish wallpaper featuring potted plants like nothing anybody in this world has ever seen, in colors they'd rather miss. There was a gas stove on spindly legs, with an oven on the right, and beyond that a lavatory-style sink. We went around the kitchen table and into his combination living room and bedroom, which seemed about half the size of the kitchen. Bookshelves lined the wall opposite a single window, and at the far end was a daybed with three cushions—the kind that has a pull-out bed on a lower level. I never could figure why they call it a daybed, when for most people it is a couch through the day and a bed at night. There was a writing desk next to a curtained-off closet at the end of the bookshelf opposite the daybed.

Tipsy told us cheerfully that living at Kellerman's was a constant party. You could hear not only the dialogue in the halls but chatter in apartments on both sides and below. One big happy family, he assured us.

"I'll bet," said Hazel, shoe-horning in her question, "that you were the leader of the band."

He grinned and asked how she guessed that.

Hazel gave him her flattering smile and said, "You strike me as the leader type. What do you play?"

"Cornet. Lots of guys in bands play trumpet, but it hasn't got the tone, you know? The black guys in the East, they like that sharper note. Me, I like it mellow."

"What'd Link play?"

"Slide trombone, tuba, even trumpet. But for our band it was the trombone. He was damned good. And quick. I mean, he hardly had to read the music once, and he had it cold."

"How'd he get along with the other guys?"

"We all got along good. It wasn't like one of those bands that play the small towns and got a couple of old farts that're always bitching and young punks that stretch the break trying to make out with some chippie in a car outside."

"We hear," I said, "that you were pretty sore when he tried to make out with Kat."

"Well, sure. We all were. What'd you expect? But we could understand, because she's a girl makes a man awful horny, and hell, she should've known better than to let him into her room when she knew he was tight. We got all that settled—he never tried again."

"He didn't have a lot of chances after that first one, did he?"

"No—"

"So how do you figure him getting pitched over the cliff there?"

"I just can't figure it at all. It doesn't make sense that Link'd go around by her place with some idea of maybe catching her around outside. He was too smart."

"You know who drove Kat home Sunday night?"

"Well, after the river trip, we were all in my car and just dropped her off. Then we went back to the motel, and everybody went their own way."

"Anybody paired up overnight?"

"Watson, Dutch, and I drove back to the Cities in my car. Chris drove Engen back to Menomonie, then drove home to Chippewa Falls. We figured Link would be going home in his Olds. End of weekend party."

I asked where he'd been born, and he said in a small town south of Milwaukee. Nolan Watson came from a farm near there, and they'd gone to the same school through the first four grades. Then Nolan's parents gave up farming and moved to Milwaukee, where his father got a job as a truck driver. They met again in high school when Tipsy's family moved to Milwaukee.

"I understand your father owns a pawnshop," I said.

His eyebrows went up. "Where'd you get that?"

"Isn't it true?"

"Yeah, but it doesn't seem like a thing a stranger'd know. I guess you've been talking with some of the band guys—"

"I've been talking with all kinds of people."

"You never talked with Link."

"That's a fact. You mind telling me a little more about him? What'd he do besides blow a trombone with your band?"

"Well, he went to classes at the U of M, chased girls, mostly had a good time."

"Kind of liked his booze, didn't he?"

"Don't we all?"

"Is Kat the only one he ever came on too strong with?"

"Far as I know, yeah. But unless he brought it up, how'd I know unless somebody raised a big stink about it?"

"You guys ever have a bet on who'd make out first with Kat?"

He shook his head and looked genuinely annoyed. "None of us ever talked about her like that. Never. We never even talked about how far we got. It wasn't something we did. Everybody knew she was more special than other girls—"

"Okay. None of the guys we've talked with ever said she was putting out. One of them said if anybody had gone the whole trip with her, it would've been you. Why'd he think that?"

"What's any of this got to do with Link getting killed?"

"That's what I'm trying to find out."

"That doesn't figure. Link's the guy got killed. He's the only guy in our crowd who tried to make her, and he got put down, so why'd anybody be jealous of him?"

"Maybe it has nothing to do with being jealous. From all we've heard, it seems like Kat's the only one of you that stayed really sore about him trying to rape her. Maybe one of you guys decided she'd really go for the one who settled his hash permanently."

"That's crazy."

"Yeah. But that's how guys get about a woman like Kat. Hasn't it ever dawned on you that she resented the guys laying off Link after a couple days of giving him a hard time?"

He wasn't about to admit that, but didn't argue the point.

"And any one of the guys, or maybe two of them, could have decided to go around and make sure Link didn't try to approach Kat at her parents' place."

"Well, I don't think anybody would've done that alone, and nobody told me they went. None of our guys would've done anything crazy as tossing him over the cliff, even if they caught him jumping Kat again."

"It might've been an accident. Somebody there had a gun. We heard it go off before he went over. Any of your band guys have one?"

"No. Absolutely not."

"How do you know?"

"I know the guys."

"Tipsy," I said, "your guys have already told us Link had a gun."

He stared at me for a few seconds, then sighed and nodded. "Okay, so he did have one. I meant none of the rest of us. Link showed his to us once. After the trouble with Kat. Like he was letting us know we shouldn't mess with him. I don't know what made him do that—nobody ever threatened him. It was a little kid kind of thing. Part of his need to seem bigger than he was." He slumped back in his chair, scowling. "I can't figure it," he admitted. "It just doesn't make sense he'd go around to her home, especially so damned late."

"What other reason would he have for going around that cliff?"

"It beats me," he admitted. "I've been thinking about it plenty. Maybe he thought if he made an approach there and buttered up the grandparents, he could convince her he wanted to marry her or something. But hell, he wouldn't try that at four in the morning. The trouble is, Link was a really sharp guy, and he got all screwed up because he wasn't able to make out like most of us in the band, and I just guess it made him a little nuts at times. I mean, in grade school he'd been the hottest thing around and got used to getting what he wanted, one way or another. Never gave up on anything he was after. You know he skipped a year of grade school? It made him awful cocky. Who knows what a guy like that will try when he's got a snoot full?"

"Somebody told us Link had a new Oldsmobile. How come it hasn't shown up around where he died?"

"How the hell would I know? Probably whoever pitched him over, took it. Likely sold it. Hey, maybe that's why he got killed. Somebody wanted the car."

"It seems funny that a guy going to school and playing only a few dance jobs along the way could buy a car like that."

"He claimed he won it in a crap game."

"Was he a regular gambler?"

"Oh, yeah. Poker, craps, pool. He'd bet on the weather."

"What's your game?"

"Solitaire," he said soberly, then grinned.

"Who was closest to him in the band?"

"Well, he and Chris did a lot of kidding during our shows, but I don't know they got together during breaks. Maybe a time or two—when they worked out something with a couple girls that were together and eager. He and Dutch Haar were both from South St. Paul, but I never saw them together. Link wasn't a cozy kind of guy. He had to outdo everybody, whether it was blowing a horn, playing cards, shooting dice, or chasing women. He managed all of those things fine, except maybe the women."

"Was he close to his family?"

"Hell, no. He even got out of his ma early. Premature by a couple weeks. Bragged about it. I figure that's the reason he took up the horn—to get out of the house and play dances. Was doing that from the time he was fourteen."

He came up with the address of Linklater's parents, which had been given to him because it was the closest thing Link had to a permanent address where people like Tipsy could reach him.

Hazel and I spent the night in a small motel at the edge of town and talked about the band members. She asked me which of the fellows said Tipsy was the most likely guy to have gone all the way with Kat. I admitted fibbing for a feeler.

"Just about like your claim that other band members admitted seeing Link's gun. You're a very tricky guy, for a cowboy type. Aren't you afraid I'll be disillusioned?"

"Nope. I don't believe you've ever been fooled by me."

She gave me a quickie kiss, backed off, and said she didn't think any of the Klan had really liked Link.

"He was a born outsider. Overcompetitive, self-centered, and always a little bit better than anybody else at everything. Maybe a lot better. Except with women."

"He wasn't too good at survival."

"But isn't it interesting—if Haar has it right—that he could always be reached through his parents? I mean, so far everything we've heard has made him sound like a complete rebel, but now it seems he must have kept that link. That doesn't seem consistent to me."

From my experience, consistency doesn't weigh much in family relations.

W e slept a little late, had breakfast in a small café, and then looked up pawnshops in the telephone directory. None carried the name Tobler, but after a couple calls, Hazel found one named Best Pawnbrokers where the man answering the phone said he was Dan Tobler.

We got to the shop a little before 11:00 A.M. It was a surprise to find that tall Tipsy's father was a tiny man with sloping shoulders, bony hands, and a small potbelly. It seemed that at least he should look like the pawnbrokers in movies, with an eyeshade and a magnifying glass practically attached to his right eye. Old Dan was bareheaded, bald, and wore rimless eyeglasses halfway down his skinny nose.

I explained that we'd been talking with his son the night before and asked if he happened to know Tipsy's friend, Link.

"My son's name is Phil," he told me with polite firmness while peering over his small glasses, "and no, I don't know any of the boys in his band. He doesn't bring them around to his old home, nor here to the shop, and I don't go dancing a whole lot."

"Have you heard what happened to his trombone player?"

"I don't know anything about him."

"He's the guy I asked about, nicknamed Link. Real name's Francis Linklater."

"I can understand why he goes by a nickname. So, is he in some kind of trouble?"

"Yeah. He's dead. He went over a cliff onto a railroad track in Wisconsin. Hasn't your son told you about that?"

He sighed, shaking his head. "Phil doesn't tell me much of anything about what goes on with his band. When did this happen?"

"Before sunup, last Monday."

He looked at me, then at Hazel, and shook his head again. "You don't look like cops, neither one of you. Why are you asking me these questions?"

"I've been hired by the mayor of the town where it happened to poke around and find out what's behind it. We were camping on the river when the body went over a cliff along the St. Croix. You sure you've never done any business with this guy Link?"

"Not that I know of, no. I can't remember ever buying or selling a trombone. As far as I know, I've never met any of the band, like I told you before. Do I look like a man who'd throw a trombone player off a cliff?"

"Not much. But somebody had a reason to kill the guy. We're shy on a motive, so all we can do is keep fishing around. He owned a car that was too damned fancy for a college boy without a good-paying job. Easy money just naturally comes to mind."

"And you figure maybe a pawnshop can be some kind of gold mine for young punks?"

I leaned against his counter and smiled at him. "I have to try all the angles. One of them in this case is the fact that this guy who got murdered had tried to rape your son's girlfriend a couple months back. She tried to get the cops on him for it, but then backed off. This is the girl who sings with Phil's band. They all pant for her, but from what we hear, your son's her favorite guy. So naturally there will be some who think that when this dude who tried to lay her showed up in her hometown, your boy Phil intercepted and tossed him off the bluff."

He took all of this in with a steady gaze that showed more skepticism than surprise, let alone shock. "Where'd all this happen?" he asked, after staring at me a second or so.

I told him.

"Phil has a full-time job here in town this summer. He couldn't have been playing bodyguard to any girl in Wisconsin."

"His band played a job Saturday night in the nearest town to where Link got killed. I guess you don't see your son too often."

"He drops in noons a lot, during his break at the clothing store. Now and then I take him out to lunch when things are quiet here. I didn't hear anything about any trip to Wisconsin."

"And he's never told you about the rape story, let alone the murder?"

"He knows I don't want to hear gossip about his damned band."

"What do you talk about?"

"Running a pawnshop, selling clothes, whatever's goin' on in the real world."

We stared at each other in silence for a moment.

"Okay," I said, "there's one other little thing we learned talking with the cops in Minneapolis. We heard Link's old man is a lawyer named Oran. And that he's been your mouthpiece."

He looked me straight in the eye and said, "Really? Well, isn't that a coincidence. I didn't even know my lawyer had a son.

When I'm paying a man by the hour, I don't waste a lot of time gabbing with him about his family."

"But maybe you know he earns enough to buy a fancy car for his kid, huh?"

"I don't doubt that a damn bit. He's made enough off of me to manage that."

14

After leaving the pawnbroker, we strolled around on Seventh Street off Nicollet Avenue to the Forum cafeteria and had lunch with the common folk. Hazel loved the place but complained when we finally sat down with our selections that she invariably took either too much or not enough where there were so many choices offered. In this case she said it was too much, but she had no problem that showed in getting it all down. I said she reminded me of myself years back, when my old man used to call me Hollow Legs because of the way I put away groceries.

Hazel agreed with me that old man Tobler had lied about how often he saw his son, probably exaggerating to set up an alibi if the young man needed it. Neither of us could figure much about him beyond that. Maybe he had been a little too strong on his lack of interest in the band. She was more inclined to believe that than I was.

After we left the cafeteria, a telephone call to Oran Linklater's office got me his secretary, who said Mr. Linklater was not in; could she take a message? She refused to give me his home number, saying she didn't believe he'd be taking any calls because there had been a death in the family. I said I knew that and was working with the mayor of the town where the death occurred to find out what had happened, so I needed to speak with the father of the victim. After considering that a second or so, she gave me the number.

Linklater answered on the second ring. When I gave him my name, he said Yes, he'd been told by the sheriff from Indeville that I'd be around. He spoke in a soft voice, as though trying to avoid waking a sleeping companion. "I understand," he said, "that you're the man who pulled Francis off the railroad track in front of the steam engine. They say you could have been killed."

"It didn't look that close to me at the time. I'd like to come out and talk with you—is that okay?"

"Of course. But give me a few moments—I drove to Indeville last night and haven't been up long. Let me give you the address." He gave me the street and number, along with simple directions, and after Hazel and I drank some coffee, we drove out, circling the block once to get the feeling of the place. Linklater's home wasn't quite a mansion, but it was larger, whiter, and had a wider, much better kept-up lot than any of its neighbors.

We climbed three steps to a broad, open porch, and before I could knock, the door opened. I'd expected to find the lawyer in a bathrobe, but he was fully dressed in a navy blue suit, white shirt, and gray tie. He even looked freshly shaved. I took in his large earlobes and the short thumbs that had been so apparent on his son. He showed no surprise at the sight of Hazel, so I guessed the sheriff had told him about her. After solemnly shaking hands with me and bowing to Hazel, he led us into a short hall and through a door on the left, which opened into a large living room with what Hazel later assured me were Persian carpets. She also told me the furniture probably came from Chicago.

He invited us to sit on the broad couch and perched on the edge of a massive easy chair in the corner.

"What can I tell you?" he asked.

"Well, it's a little hard to say. How'd you and your son get on?"

He stared at me for a moment, then slid back in the chair and folded his hands in his lap.

"When he was little, we got on very well. Of course in those days I was just beginning my practice and wasn't home a lot. Most of the time, in the beginning, he got along beautifully with his mother, who always let him have his way. He was so quick and clever he managed her easily from the time he was weaned. I think I realized early on that she was spoiling him, but I didn't worry about it because we had so little contact and he was so small I felt very tolerant. But things changed when he got bigger and started junior high school. By then I had a little better control of my time and was free weekends, and I could see how out of hand he'd become. Worse, I sensed that he had very little respect for his mother. So I began a little program of getting him straightened out. He was doing so well in school that the idea of him coming into the firm with me seemed like a great prospect, and I tried to guide him in that direction. At first he seemed to accept my taking charge, but gradually I could sense he was pulling away, and almost as soon as he started high school, he let me know he wasn't even vaguely interested in law as a career. Thinking back now, I try to take what satisfaction I can from the fact I never even attempted to dictate his course in life. When he wanted to become a musician, I paid for the instruments he thought he needed and provided funds for music lessons. Frankly, I thought it was something he'd outgrow, and I didn't mind indulging his fancies, since I could afford it."

It seemed more than likely he'd minded in the worst way. He was busy being a lawyer, making a case for himself.

"How old was he when he last lived with you?" I asked.

He frowned, to let me know he was thinking. "Well, I guess it was up till he went to college—"

"It was when he was sixteen," said a voice from the hall doorway.

We looked around to take in Linklater's wife. She was slender, with gray-streaked hair brushed straight, framing her haggard, pale face. Her red lipstick looked like a fresh scar, and she examined me from behind thick-lensed glasses that made her eyes owly. She looked as if she hadn't slept for days. "That," she said, "was when he got a job playing with a dance band twice a week. Oh, he came home often enough to bring his clothes for washing and pick up fresh, and a few times he ate lunches with me. The rest of the time he stayed at a boardinghouse owned by one of the band members."

"That wasn't the band he was with this last year, was it?" I asked.

"No. It was a different bunch. I forget the name. He was only with them a year."

"This is my wife," said Linklater, "Marilyn. These are the Wilcoxes, Hazel and Carl."

We greeted each other, and she sat down across from us in a straight-backed chair. She didn't look at her husband but, after her first words to me, turned her eyes on Hazel. "Did you know him?" she asked.

Hazel shook her head.

Linklater leaned toward his wife. "These are the people that found Francis on the tracks. Mr. Wilcox pulled Francis from in front of the steam engine."

"I don't want to hear about that," she said, and got up and walked out.

Linklater sighed, sat back, and apologized for his wife. "She can't handle this," he said. "She's about out of her mind with grief."

"That's easy to understand," said Hazel. "Carl, we should leave."

Linklater waved his hand, vaguely. "It's all right. I have to face all of this, and there's no point in it getting dragged out forever. You want to know what I know about my son, and it's damned embarrassing having to face the fact I knew so little. He was always a problem child. You see, being more intelligent than any of his classmates, he had little respect for them or their ways, and couldn't tolerate their limitations. It was a little encouraging, when he first joined that band group, that they were generally misfits, almost matching him. That girl Katarina was the first who really challenged him—they were much alike in many ways—so apart from their peers, so to speak. I think it made them attractive to each other, but it also set them up as rivals. Do you understand that? That business of him trying to make love to her, it was his attempt to assert his male superiority, you know? He'd never have gone that far sober, but he found sobriety so limiting, I suspect, he couldn't stay with it."

"Did he tell you anything about Kat and the band?"

"Not really. He told his mother quite a bit, and she passed it on to me. Marilyn never questioned him when he bragged, and he only talked about the band to let us both know he was doing well and having a great time."

"Did you buy him the car he had?"

He smiled cozily. "How'd you happen to ask that? What have you heard?"

"That he won it in a crap game. Only nobody seems to know where or exactly when."

"Well, it's a little embarrassing, but I'll have to admit, I

helped him out there. It was a tough decision—I worried about
him driving since he drank so much—but he almost never asked
me for anything, and when this came up, I suppose I thought it
was an opportunity to win him over a bit, and I wanted him to
have a good, safe car. Lord knows he couldn't have paid for one
himself, whatever claims he made to his friends about his gambling talents. So one afternoon we went over to Eau Claire and
bought this used car from the widow of a fellow who had died of
a heart attack."

"What was her name?" I asked.

"I've no idea—something very common, like Johnson, I
think."

"You pay by check?"

"Oh, no. I'd been putting aside a cash reserve for several
years, planning to buy a car for him as a graduation present. So
he talked me into making it a bit in advance. Speaking of the car,"
he said, straightening up, "I understand it's missing. Has it occurred to anyone that he could've been murdered by someone
who stole it?"

"It's one of the angles the sheriff's working on. The big
question is still, how'd he happen to be in Kat Bacon's territory
when he got killed? He'd already been in big trouble for crowding
her—why'd he suddenly head out her way that night?"

"I'm afraid it's completely in character. Nothing increased
Francis's aggressiveness like rejection or failure. Does this Bacon
girl deny he tried to arrange to meet her that night?"

"I haven't asked her yet. Didn't know until recently that the
band had been in town that weekend."

"Well, I'd think if he did try to arrange anything with her,
she'd have volunteered that information."

"Not if she was afraid it might get somebody thinking she
had something to do with his murder."

Linklater almost managed a tolerant smile. "Of course. I have the impression that neither you nor any of the others interested in this case have ever considered that this Kat girl may have been carrying a grudge because she felt that Francis had treated her as if she were a tramp. Maybe she lured him into her town and had him ambushed. Stranger things happen these days."

Once we were back in our car, Hazel asked if I'd noticed what a different Link we saw from the father's point of view, compared to what the band guys told us.

"Like all the talk about his son being pushy when crossed? Yeah, that hit me too. Like he was trying to make the kid into something he could accept better. Just generally, the way a lawyer's mind works has always knocked me out."

"You mean, like trying to blame the victim?"

"Yeah."

"Well, Carl, you should know that when a woman's involved, that's generally how men's minds work."

When I scowled at her, she grinned. "I suppose," she said, "I should have made that *some* men—"

We headed back toward Indeville in the afternoon and had dinner with Sheriff Steiger and Deputy Dewey. They agreed with me that the trip hadn't rewarded us much, but Dewey liked the idea of another visit with Kat—preferably well away from the grandparents. I asked if Dewey knew whether Kat ever went to the Saturday-night dances when she was still in high school. He said yes, he'd seen her there with Priscilla several times. He couldn't remember her getting involved with any particular guys back then.

"Fine," I said, turning to Hazel. "So we'll try to catch her there tomorrow night. Meanwhile, we'll get up early in the morning and take a trip to Foxton—look up the widow of the guy that died in his basement this spring."

"What's on your mind?"

"Nothing special. Just want to hear what the lady might have to say."

Hazel looked wise. "Let's go," she said.

he Foxton cop looked ancient as my old man Elihu and just about as frisky. His name was Conklin Mertz. He told me to call him Conk. Sure, he knew where I could find Nate Pryke's widow. He also told me the widow had taken back her maiden name, Iverson. Her first name was Carmen.

"She's been the soda jerk at Pop's ice cream parlor on Main Street ever since she was widowed this spring," he told us. "It wasn't like she needed the job, you know. Her father-in-law's loaded and anything but stingy. Takes care of her yet. But she ain't the kind to sit home and moon around, likes to gad about."

"Kind of loose?" I asked.

"Well now, I didn't say that. She's not a bad girl. Maybe a little perkier than most, that's all."

Carmen Iverson Pryke was alone reading a magazine behind the counter when we entered the soda fountain. She quickly stuffed it out of sight and worked up a smile. She was slim as a doe, taller than average, and wore her pale red hair short and close to her head. Her blue eyes were wide apart and bright. We took one of the small round tables nearest her, and Hazel said she'd have an ice cream soda. I asked for root beer.

"Just passing through?" asked Carmen as she fixed our orders.

"Yeah," I said. "Dropped in here to ask directions, in a way."

She raised one thin eyebrow, carried our glasses over, and placed them in front of us. "In a way?"

"Yeah. I'm trying to find out how and why a guy got murdered in your neighbor town. Fella named Francis Linklater. Everybody called him Link. You hear about it?"

She straightened up and stared at me a couple seconds before answering, and I suspected she was going to play dumb. But then she took a deep breath and nodded. "Of course I heard about it. Everybody's been talking about it and asking questions. I even knew him a little. What I don't understand is, why anybody'd think it was murder. Couldn't he have just fallen off that cliff? He drank a lot, you know."

"We don't think so. Besides, there was a shot, too. How well did you know him?"

She shrugged and made a negative mouth. "It didn't amount to anything. Danced with him a few times, and he took me along to that little party the band guys threw for Kat. She resented me. Didn't think any of the band should ever pay attention to any girl but her. She was *really* peeved that he brought me to her special party."

"Did Link ever talk about her to you?"

"No. He hardly talked to me at all. The whole business between us was kind of weird. Why're you asking me these questions? You think I'm the kind of girl who could have pushed him over a cliff just because he used me to spite Kat?"

"How'd he do that?"

"He invited me to that party the band had for her, and I could tell right off that he was watching her all the time he was making up to me, while she tried to pretend I didn't exist. One of the other boys in the band told me how Link had tried to do her and she got mad. You know all about that, I suppose."

"Yeah, we heard. But the reason we wanted to talk with you is, you're the only lady around here I've heard of that was close to another guy who died sudden just lately. The cops in Indeville claim your husband's death left a lot of questions."

She drew back, looking so shook up I right away told her they didn't suspect her—her alibi checked out fine, and she wasn't in any trouble. What we were after was some notion as to why anybody might want her husband dead, because we figured it was possible there was a connection between his death and the one we were investigating.

She seemed a little reassured but said that, frankly, she was blamed tired of talking and thinking about the whole mess. Everybody had been into it for what seemed like a year.

Hazel asked how she happened to get the job in the soda fountain.

Carmen smiled for the first time since we showed up. Her teeth were a little big but pretty even, framed by full lips and a wide mouth.

"That was simple—Pop, the owner, is my uncle. When he heard about my husband dying, he talked me into taking this job right off, to give me something to take my mind off my tragedy. He swore he needed help right away or he couldn't stay in business. So I pretended to believe him and took it on. He's really sweet."

She liked talking about her uncle and made the old man sound like a saint. Switching to him loosened her up enough so after a few moments it seemed okay to steer things back to the question of her husband, and I asked her to tell us about their life together.

She said at the time Nate got killed, they had been into their third year of farming. Nate's grandfather, who was a wealthy banker in the East, had bought the farm and kept them supplied with cash to live on, but it turned out to be a nightmare. Nate knew nothing about farming, was shy about asking for help from neighbors, and had no luck with hired hands. They could barely raise food for their own meals, let alone produce profitable crops. The grandfather kept sending money, so they had no trouble eating regularly, but the failure got to Nate, and he started drinking hard. At first it was just on weekends, but soon it was every day. She nagged at him to stop, and they fought almost daily—mostly talk, except once when he actually slapped her. It wasn't hard, and later he was terribly ashamed and apologetic. She admitted that one morning she had taken a swing at him with the rolling pin, but luckily only caught his forearm and not his head. Nearly all of the abuse, she claimed, was in bad-mouthing, and she confessed she'd done most of it until finally she just gave up on him. She cooked him meals and went her own way. He didn't seem to care. He had never been a deeply loving or overpossessive man, and never worried what people said about him or her.

When she learned about his death and came home, she discovered that the cash box he kept stored in their closet had disappeared. She claimed she had no idea how much might have been in it, but she knew that he kept money there because he didn't trust the banks after so many had gone broke. This was money sent by his grandfather every month. He had never told Carmen how much it amounted to, but she thought it had been fairly generous because they never seemed short despite the farm failure.

She told us that a few days before his death, Nate had passed the word around the area that they had a tractor to sell. He had never been able to make the one they got with the farm work, and he hadn't the foggiest notion of how to repair it. He hoped some mechanic in the territory would believe he could fix it.

"This gun that your husband was holding when he was found—had you seen it before?" I asked.

"Yes, of course. He kept it out in the barn and used to take pot shots at gophers now and then."

"Maybe somebody shot your husband because he caught them going through your house," said Hazel.

Carmen said that was what the sheriff thought. He figured somebody had answered the ad Nate ran, and while one man was out with Nate by the tractor, a partner had been prowling through the house. Then maybe something made Nate suspicious or he got needing a drink and went back inside and caught the thief in the act, and the two fellows killed him and arranged it to look like a suicide. She said that incidentally, the tractor was still on the farm.

I asked if when she'd been with Link, she ever could tell whether he'd carried a gun, or maybe noticed he had one in his car. She said no, certainly not.

"Did you see him that Sunday night before he died?"

She shook her head emphatically.

We thanked her, paid up, and left.

At the gas station I questioned the man who filled my tank, and he said yes, he'd known the murdered man—pumped gas for him many times. Yes, he allowed that Nate was a pretty heavy drinker, but so far as he knew, he hadn't chased, let alone caught, any women around town. The only fellow he could think of who might have been considered close to Nate in the territory was his immediate farm neighbor, Clarence Quinn.

Quinn's farm was on land so low it even had a slough on the north end, with brackish water and a few mudhens paddling about. From the look of it, they may simply have been wading; the water didn't look deep enough for swimming.

The farmhouse needed paint and could have stood some propping up—it looked like a good sneeze would flatten the sagging front porch. We found the farmer tentatively digging up red potatoes around back. He had a high forehead, a dimpled chin, and surprisingly clean overalls. He greeted us with the kind of attention I was getting used to in company with Hazel. After a little chatter about who we were and what we were after, he invited us into the house, where his short and chubby wife was nursing a baby, who she introduced us to as Nelly. Nelly, who showed no signs of undernourishment, also showed no interest in strangers and stayed with the nipple. The mother finished with the feeding, tucked herself away, put the baby in a basket on the floor, and set the coffeepot on the range.

The husband never called his wife anything but Ma, and I didn't push for more, but Hazel wouldn't hold still for that and asked her name. She smiled and said it was Honoria but most people just called her Hon, like in honey. Once the baby was sound asleep, Hon showed great interest in the only murder in their lives.

"I won't pretend I was terribly fond of Nate, but you couldn't help feeling sorry for him because when you got down to it, he was really just an overgrown kid. Had no more business trying to run a farm than I would, and always truckled to his rich grandpa, who dominated him all his life."

"How'd Carmen react to his murder?" asked Hazel.

"Well, we—or I should say, I—never had any real contact with her. Clarence had a little. We know that after she found the body, she just packed up and left the place. Far as we heard, she's never gone back. Her uncle, the one everybody calls Pop, had to make the funeral arrangements and wired the grandfather—his name is Gideon, of all things—and he came and actually stayed at the farm a night or so and arranged to sell it and got Carmen moved into a little apartment in town. Actually I'm not all that sure he really sold the house, but he set her up comfortably. She took the job Pop offered because she needed something to do and she likes meeting people—I'm sure it wasn't because she needed the money. The old grandfather enjoys running people, you know, but prefers doing it from a distance, I think."

"How'd people accept Carmen after the murder?"

"Well, mostly they were pretty nice. Sure, there are a few

folks claim she didn't care a fig for Nate back when he was alive, since she was always running around to dances and things—but for goodness sake, *he* didn't mind, so why should anybody else make a fuss?"

"Did she start going back to the dance halls right after he died?"

"Oh, no. It was at least a month or so."

"Where'd she go dancing?"

"All around. Menomonie, Indeville, and anyplace else in reach, to listen to the bands and dance with all the stags on Saturday nights and even Wednesdays. Nate always used to take her to them, but wouldn't set foot on the dance floor. Mostly he'd go someplace and get tanked up. I suspect he had two left feet."

"Didn't he get jealous about her running around?"

"If he did, he never let anyone know about it. Everybody knew he'd go to the dance hall with her and buy her ticket, so he couldn't have been all that bothered. To tell the truth, all I know is stories I've heard from some of my Ladies Aid friends."

"Did those friends ever mention Carmen getting cozy with any guys in one of the bands?"

"Of course. They said she was always making eyes at them and talking with them between numbers."

"Anybody claim she went out on breaks with these guys?"

"Oh, yes. I'm not convinced any of them know anything for sure, but the church folks all love to think Carmen's a loose woman. It gives them lots to talk about and shake their heads over. The way I figure it, Carmen's just crazy about music and the people that make it. I don't think she's all that nuts about, you know, fooling around. I mean, seriously."

"How'd she get around to neighboring towns after her husband was dead?"

"Her grandfather-in-law bought her a Shove-it-or-Leave-it,

LEAD, SO I CAN FOLLOW | 97

you know, a Chevrolet, when he was here for the funeral. She had sold Nate's car after he died but later was sorry and let old Gideon know."

I asked Quinn if he could tell me anything about Nate Pryke. He hemmed and hawed a bit before allowing as how he was a nice guy who had needed help. The trouble was, he would never come out and ask for it, and who could figure what the hell he really needed?

"When his grandpa first set him up, he used to come over and ask me for advice, but before long, we just wound up gabbing. He told me all about this grandpa of his who was a big banker in New York and made piles of money and had worked from the time he was like maybe thirteen. And all his life the old man talked about how he'd someday buy a farm and manage it the way his father had in the old country. He had this dopey notion that a farmer had fun and the land just fed him and was there to look at and admire. All he had to do was work a bit when he pleased and then coast through the winter, drinking coffee and jawing with his wife and kids.

"Nate learned quick that it was nothing like that, and he let his grandpa know it, but the old man told him to stick with it, he'd supply the cash to live on, and eventually he'd learn the ropes and be in clover. When Nate tried to convince him it wasn't going to work, he should do something else, the old man got ornery and made it plain it was farm or he'd cut off the monthly check, so Nate hung on and hired help when he could get it. Quinn suspected that Carmen, who began having fun when she started flirting around, didn't want that sure check to stop coming and added her pressures to keep Nate where he was."

"You ever get any idea how much money Nate got from his grandpa?"

"No. He was real shy about that. Hon figures he lied to

Carmen about how much it was, so she wouldn't hound him for more than she got for buying groceries and what clothes she had. He hardly ever gave her cash but was always willing to buy whatever she asked for. She got lots of clothes and small jewelry."

"Did the grandfather ever come to visit?"

"Oh, you bet. Came one Christmas, and he was quite a surprise. He's a hunchback, walks with two canes when he's not riding a wheelchair. Almost a midget, you know? He's real tiny, but he's got more get-up-and-go than a bull with a hard-on. Wears real neat clothes, always a white shirt and a fine tie—silk, I bet. Got thin white hair. Came around after Nate shot himself and looked up the sheriff, and later talked with the mayor. I figured he's never believed Nate shot himself. Neither the sheriff nor the mayor told anybody what they talked about. But the old man's a real character, believe me. Nothing he'd do would surprise me much."

On the way back to our motel I asked Hazel if she thought that the reason the mayor offered us money to help run this case down was because maybe he had met the grandfather Gideon Pryke when he came for the funeral of his grandson, and figured the old man might pay off any expenses of an investigation. She told me I certainly had a nasty mind, and yes, she figured I was right.

e drifted around to the dance hall about half past nine that evening. It was hot out, so of course it was hotter still in the dance hall, despite the big fan blowing huffily in a corner near the open back door. We didn't spot Kat anywhere around, and I had the same luck when rubbernecking for Carmen. Hazel suggested we dance, and I went along since it wasn't too tricky a number for me to handle. About halfway through, Hazel leaned close and whispered, "Kat's with us."

So she was, as well as Chris Christenson and Skinny Engen, the two band guys from neighboring towns. They were in a huddle not far from the bandstand. When the number ended, all three of them drifted over and started talking with the leader, a chubby guy, who played an alto sax.

They got a couple laughs before the band struck up the next number, which was "I'm in the Mood for Love." Chris and Kat danced to it, and so did we. I worked us over beside the young couple. Kat spotted us first. Her face, for just a second, showed something between fear and what for her might be anger; then she spoke to her partner and managed a big smile our way as he turned to look. Chris's expression was strictly deadpan; he simply nodded in acknowledgment.

Not being coy, I moved in as casually as my style allowed and told Kat I'd like to talk with her again. Chris, smooth as a movie star, said no time like the present, and offered to trade partners.

We managed the switch with only me losing the beat temporarily, and for a few seconds I concentrated strictly on adjusting to Kat's style. The primary switch was hers, since she was much more talented. Once it was made, I got to the point. "Did Link try to meet with you on that last weekend?" I asked.

"Of course not. He knew very well I wouldn't have gone to a church picnic with him."

"Who was his closest buddy in the band?"

She frowned prettily for a second and decided that would be Chris. They sat next to each other on every job and kidded a lot back and forth. A couple times she heard they had double-dated with girls picked up on the road.

"When did Link first get involved with Carmen?"

She pulled her head back slightly and met my eyes. "What difference does that make?"

"I'm trying to find out. Was it before her husband died?"

She shrugged. "That's something I wouldn't know. Before he tried to rape me, he wouldn't have bragged any about other women, and none of the fellows ever talked to me about things like that."

"But having known her in school, you'd have noticed her hanging around. So how far back was it?"

She shrugged and said it probably was early in the fall, the first time they'd gone to Menomonie for a Saturday-night dance.

"Was that before the husband shot himself?"

"I guess so. If that's what really happened."

"Well, it doesn't sound too unnatural. Failed farmer, alcoholic, and a wife with a roving eye."

"From all I've ever heard, he didn't care about that."

"Did you figure Link was making out with her right from the start?"

"It seemed pretty likely. She made passes at anybody that blew a horn, beat a drum, or plucked the strings. A real camp follower."

"Did she go on breaks with Link, or anybody else?"

"Of course. None of the band ever told me about what or who they did on breaks. I wasn't supposed to know they ever did anything with any girl. They liked to pretend I was the only one they really wanted. That didn't make me blind to what was really going on."

"But you pretended you were?"

She laughed. "Of course, but I'm not silly enough to think they were fooled."

"You recognized the dead man was Link, didn't you?"

She turned totally sober, almost sad, and moved with me in silence for a few seconds before answering.

"I suppose so, really. But I just couldn't make myself admit it. The awfullest thing is, when he tried to force me, I wanted to kill him." She drew back a little and looked into my eyes for a second, then lowered her head. "Before that night, I'd convinced myself that all the fellows really thought I was something special. Link's treating me like a tramp just killed me. He kept telling me, while I tried to fight him off, that it was what *I* wanted. God!"

"How come you didn't report the attempted rape the night he tried it?"

She blushed and frowned. "Well, I'd stopped him, hadn't I? So he hadn't really done it."

"Then why'd you call the cops in the morning?"

Her face twisted angrily. "Because he lied about me to the guys. He told them I let him into my bed."

"So how come you withdrew the charges?"

"Well, the police were snotty about me calling the morning after, and besides, I got thinking how the other fellas wouldn't want me pushing this thing because it might get in the newspapers and hurt the band, so I gave it up."

"Do you know if any of the guys ever threatened Link if he made another try at you?"

"Well, they certainly never threatened to throw him off a cliff. But they did let him know he couldn't stay with the band if he tried anything like that again. You know something? I don't believe any of them really blamed him. Tipsy told me what happened was a good share my fault—that I was really dumb to let Link into my room that night, which was just asking for trouble. I couldn't accept that. I never led him or any of them on. Not one bit. I honestly liked them all, like brothers, and completely trusted them. I never flirted seriously—you know what I mean? I didn't sit showing my legs, or rub up against any of the guys or give them come-on looks the way loose girls do. I laughed at their jokes and told them they were great musicians and wonderful guys, because I really believed they were, and we were just a very happy family, right up until Link spoiled it all."

"Last Sunday night, when all of your gang went canoeing on the river, who was teamed up with you?"

"Well, I was in a canoe with Tipsy and Jan—"

"Jan?"

"Jan Haar. The fellows call him Dutch, but I don't."

"Oh, yeah, I forgot. So where was Link?"

"All I really know is, he didn't go on the river with us. I just supposed he was off messing around with that Carmen woman. The other canoe had Chris, Skinny, and Nolan in it. Skinny, who usually plays drums, had a guitar along and sat in the middle of their canoe and played a lot, and I sang some. It was all just lovely."

"When it was over, who took you home?"

"Tipsy and Jan."

"What time was that?"

"Oh, I suppose it was near midnight."

"Was anybody surprised that Link hadn't gone on the river with the gang?"

"Nobody said anything about it."

She told me what they talked about was plans for the coming year. The only reference to Link had been Chris's report that Link mentioned he might be getting a job with a bigger band and dropping out of the U. Tipsy was the only one who had seemed seriously worried about that. Yes, she admitted, there had been some drinking. She'd had a little beer, but the fellows were all drinking rum and Cokes, and they had quite a few. She insisted they had all stayed together the whole time, and strongly denied that she had seen or heard anything from Link the night he went over the cliff.

The saddest thing, Hazel told me when we were together later, was that Kat probably believed she had never led the fellows on too far. "I think," she said, "that our Kat is pure phony from the start, even to herself. She really wanted them all panting, and she worked at it because she wanted them all to herself. And I don't doubt she might have tried to get Link back from Carmen with promises if he showed up out at the farm."

I told her she was as tough on Kat as Kat was on Carmen. "How come women are so down on each other? Don't they get enough of that from guys?"

"We see through each other," she said. "And we only make allowances for ourselves. Something we have in common with men. Were you surprised Carmen never showed up tonight?"

"Nope. She may be a little loose, but I don't think she's stupid."

hen Oran Linklater was in Indeville, he had made arrangements to ship his son's body home for a funeral in South St. Paul. The sheriff was satisfied with the identification by then, so there was no problem there.

I left Hazel at the hotel on Sunday and drove to Foxton for another visit with Carmen, only to learn that she wasn't around. Her uncle said she'd asked for a couple days off and had persuaded a friend to fill in for her at the ice cream parlor. The substitute told me that Carmen had gone to see her dad in Eau Claire because he wasn't feeling well, and she was worried about him.

Back in Indeville I managed a conference with the mayor and Sheriff Steiger. The sheriff told me that he'd made no progress trying to find Link's car because no one knew the license number, although somewhere along the line they had been told it was a Wisconsin plate.

"Do you suppose," asked the mayor, "that the two band fellas from near here will be traveling together to the funeral for Link in Minneapolis, and maybe give Katarina a ride?"

Sheriff Steiger said he could ask, but what difference would it make?

"Well, if any of them were in on this death, it'd give them a lovely chance to discuss alibis and so forth. What if our man Carl here, and his wife, were to ride with them? We could sort of offer them a deal, like paying for travel expenses, if the group went together. Then Carl could work on them a bit during the ride, maybe learn something useful. Doesn't that make sense?"

The sherif's face showed plainly he thought it made none, but he agreed to talk with Kat and see if she could arrange it. Nobody asked for my opinion on the matter.

Hazel made a throat-clearing sound, and the two guys looked at her. "What if they don't want us along?" she asked.

The mayor smiled. "In that case, I'd make a point of how, at this stage in the investigation, we could actually refuse to let people involved leave the area if they didn't cooperate fully."

"Well, now," fussed the sheriff, "I'm not sure we could make that stick—"

"We can make them think we could, if we go about it right. You just leave it to me. I'll talk with Cole Bacon and Kat."

Neither Kat nor the mayor ever gave us any details on his conference with her, but the old politician obviously made his case because, after a telephone call to Chris Christenson, the deal was settled. We would never know for sure whether it was cash, fear, or curiosity that clinched it.

Hazel and I were left with a day on our own, and I suggested we find out where Carmen's dad lived and see if we could talk some more with Carmen. A call to Foxton's cop, Conk Mertz, got me the name of her old man, Rufus Iverson, and even his address in Eau Claire. It was a trip of nearly three hours over well-kept graveled roads that wove their way through valleys and green hills and across creeks. I told Hazel that if Minnesota was the land of lakes, Wisconsin was creek heaven.

I got directions to the Iverson address from a gas station attendant while refueling the car, and it was late afternoon when we pulled up behind a shining black Packard parked in front of a duplex with an enclosed front porch and an aged white paint job. That classy car didn't look much more out of place than a pearl necklace on a panhandler.

"What have we here?" asked Hazel as we got out and gave the Packard admiring looks.

"I'd guess it was the rich cripple from New York—why don't we go up and find out?"

My knock was answered quickly by a tall dude in a black suit who at first ignored Hazel and stared at me. He was a masterful starer, with heavy black eyebrows, dark eyes, and a tough chin.

"Yeah?" He managed to make the question sound like an accusation. "We want to see Rufus Iverson," Hazel told him quickly to keep me from growling.

He looked at her and was suddenly a smiler. "And who would you be?"

"Carl Wilcox's wife, Hazel. Is Mr. Pryke visiting here?"

That guess didn't seem to surprise the man. He gave her a still broader smile, and asked what made her think that.

"Well, the car out front is from New York. It's a little grand for this neighborhood, so it occurs to me that Carmen's grand-father-in-law may have decided to visit."

"And you're the pair that found the body on the tracks, eh? Okay, come on in."

We passed through the bare porch to the inner door and were immediately in a small living room with rag rugs, heavy pale brown curtains, and well-worn furniture. The couch had wooden arms and sagging cushions, and the floor lamp's shade was slightly crooked and bent to one side. One glance at the old man sitting in the corner chair was enough to tell me it was Gideon Pryke. His suit was a light gray that nearly glowed. He sat leaning forward, small as a child, and his thin, bony hands clutched the shaft of a cane topped with a silver ram's head almost as big as a baseball. His examining eyes were bright and wide, a deep blue, behind thick-lensed glasses. I could see he was hunchbacked. His black shoes had a bright shine. On the corner of the couch, close to Pryke, was a bulky old man with watery eyes and a large paunch. He wore brown corduroy pants and a dark blue flannel shirt, and slumped on the cushions, watching Pryke, not us. Carmen was not in sight.

"So," said the little man, "you're Carl Wilcox, the fellow who took the time to climb a cliff and find the body of a murdered man while honeymooning. Wasn't that rather out of the way under the circumstances?"

"After hearing the shot and scream, it seemed natural at the time."

"You must be a very energetic man."

"Maybe he was just inspired," said Hazel.

The bright blue eyes sparkled.

The man who'd answered the door said that Hazel had guessed who owned the car out front. Gideon Pryke leaned a little farther forward, bracing against the cane.

"Why do you think I came here?" he asked her.

"Well, since it's pretty late for the funeral of your grandson, I'd guess it was because his death still bothers you, and you've come to check up on it."

The old man looked at me. "It seems you've married quite a female Watson."

"You didn't think I picked her just for her good looks, did you?"

He smiled again and asked her what role she had figured for the man who let us in. Hazel glanced at him, standing near the door, watching with a tolerant smile of his own. "He's probably a hired companion, something more than a chauffeur or body servant. Maybe a male nurse."

Pryke chuckled and nodded. "Close. He has, in the past few weeks, been all of those things. This is Ronald Rochford, jack-of-all-trades, son of an old business partner of mine. I brought him along to help me look into my grandson's murder. The new death makes me more suspicious than ever about what happened to my nephew, and I'm quite intrigued that local people seem to share my suspicions now. That's easy to understand, isn't it?"

I nodded.

"It's all very interesting to me. From preliminary discussions with the sheriff, we have the impression that this man killed on the river somehow came into enough money to buy a new car not long after my nephew died. Have you come here suspecting that perhaps the widow knows who might have killed her husband, and that maybe she knows something tying that death to this one?"

I allowed as how it seemed like he wasn't a bad Sherlock himself, and asked where Carmen was.

"She's at the grocery store, getting something for our dinner."

"I guess you don't think she had anything to do with your grandson's killing," I said.

"Don't think for a moment the notion never occurred to me. But her father here," he said, tipping his head toward the old man on the couch, "swears she was with him at the time of the death, and there's been nothing else to go on that makes me suspect her. Over the years I've learned more about her than you might expect. I'm quite convinced she's not capable of making arrangements for her husband's death. She's basically a very simple girl, not deep or devious, a child who wants a good time and a lot of attention. Despite this, she's no fool. She knew how I felt about Nate, and that I would take care of them as long as she stayed by him despite his weaknesses. She had security, and since he never objected to her having a good time, she could do as she pleased. There was no reason for her to get rid of him."

"Could he have had a big stash in his farmhouse?" I asked.

"Well, he certainly didn't squander all I sent him on liquor or presents for his wife. I'm quite sure he had a nest egg more than sufficient to pay for a new car for any hoodlum that robbed his house. Nate was inclined to ask me for help to buy equipment quite often, and on more than one occasion, he asked for money for things, like a tractor to replace the one that broke down, but somehow he never got around to buying it. Nate was not the sort of man to have a checking account. He was suspicious of banks and was only comfortable with cash. Generally he had little self-confidence and was haunted by fears that he'd make a wrong choice. I never begrudged him that sort of thing. I knew he was having very serious problems with the farm and wanted him to feet secure, whatever happened."

I looked at Carmen's father. He had watery eyes and a sagging mouth and jaw. When Hazel gently asked him if he thought his daughter had been happy with her husband, he stirred to life, straightened up a bit, and even squared his jaw some. "She was very fond of Nate," he said. His hoarse voice was little more than a whisper. "Carmen's always been a loving girl. Always. She took good care of her husband, I don't care what anybody says. He understood her and was grateful. She always fed him regular and kept the house up real nice. A hard worker and a good girl."

A perfect wife, no matter how many men she screwed in cars or motels.

"She ever talk to you about any of the guys she messed with?" I asked.

"She never offered, and I never asked. If her husband didn't mind, why should I? Nobody ever came around gossiping about her to me. Nate never complained. Not once."

"Will you be attending the funeral of the Linklater man?" Gideon asked us.

I said yes.

"Well, when that's taken care of, get back in touch, eh? I have a proposition I'd like to talk over with you."

"Why not now?"

He smiled. "I have a couple things to take care of first. All in good time."

The funeral was scheduled for the afternoon. Chris and Skinny Engen showed up at the Bacon home, picked up Kat around ten, then drove over to our motel and stopped for us.

The trip from Indeville to the Twin Cities began over hills and winding roads offering a great variety of greenery, and we saw relatively few large stretches of corn, wheat, alfalfa, or any of the other crops so familiar in South Dakota when there was enough rain to make any of it grow. Chris was a steady driver, keeping the speedometer on fifty any time we weren't held up by traffic ahead on hilly roads. We had none of the problem I knew so well in my home territory, where dust from any car ahead of you could become blinding. It was warm enough so he had the windows rolled down, making it hard to hear talk from the front seat. Kat and Chris talked softly between themselves as we got under way. After a while I leaned forward and asked if they had any theories on Link's death. Kat turned halfway around and said she simply couldn't let herself think about any of it. Chris kept his eyes on the road ahead. All of the conversation that followed was in high volume, while Hazel and I leaned forward with our jaws practically resting on the seatbacks before us.

"I just guess somebody wanted his stash," Chris told us. "What else have you got?"

"Not much. At least not in this company. Nobody wants to talk about the attempted rape of Kat here. It's kind of stretching coincidence that this guy died more or less in her backyard."

"Oh, come on—" said Chris, "that was nothing to bring on murder, for God's sake."

I wished I could see Kat's reaction, but she just looked ahead, and I couldn't catch a view from my angle in the mirror.

"Do any of you know how he got that car he had?" Hazel asked.

"He claimed he won it in a crap game," said Chris. "Told us it was after we played a dance in Menomonie."

"When was that?"

Chris shrugged. "About a couple months back."

"So none of you guys were with him at that game?" I asked.

"No. The rest of us were always too pooped after a job to spend hours at a crap game or poker table. But playing his horn always got Link hopped up, and he couldn't sleep right away, so if he didn't have a girl he went looking for a game. I've no idea how or where he found them."

"I don't believe that story," said Kat. "Where, in Menomonie, would you find an all-night dice game?"

"Maybe in a hotel," said Chris, "or even somebody's home. You don't know about guys like that."

"Thank God," said Hazel to me as we both settled back and gave up trying to outshout the wind.

After a moment I leaned forward a little and looked at Skinny Engen, who was on the far side of Hazel. "How about you? Any ideas?"

"Afraid not." He looked so innocent it naturally made me suspicious.

"Did you know Carmen Pryke?" Hazel asked.

He glanced at the back of Kat's head and saw she was leaning toward Chris, who was talking to her so low we couldn't hear. Skinny turned our way slightly. "Sure, we all did. She showed up at the dances we played in Wisconsin and hung around the band-stand a lot."

"Who'd she seem most interested in?"

"Well, I guess that'd be Link, because he paid her a lot of attention, but she looked us all over." He grinned modestly. "Even me."

"She interest you?"

He glanced toward Kat again before answering, "Sure, why not?"

"Did you think she was hoping to score with one of you guys during intermission?"

"Well, yeah, she gave all the guys big ideas. But then when we had our little party for the band, and Carmen showed up with Link, that was a surprise to all of us because, well, we knew Kat didn't like her, and hell, this was a party for Kat."

"Where was this party held?"

"In the beer parlor next to the dance hall. They've got this room in back of the main lounge for private parties."

"Was this a good-bye thing?" asked Hazel. "Did you guys all think maybe the band wouldn't get together again in the fall?"

"Oh yeah, that was a part of it. It seemed like chances were we couldn't all get back into the same apartment building again, and Link had been talking about how he might drop out of school. This other band he played for a few times in June and July was bigger than ours and got fatter payoffs. Link didn't figure he could work with them and still go to the U."

"Did he make that much difference to your band?"

Skinny shrugged. "He was good as anybody we had, but he gave us a lot of headaches too, like coming back late from breaks and causing trouble sometimes because he'd work too hard on one of the girls that hung around, and that'd make the local boys sore."

He glanced toward the front seat again. Kat had moved a bit away from Chris and slumped down far enough to rest her head on the edge of the seatback.

Skinny leaned a fraction closer to Hazel before going on.

"Kat wasn't the only one he came on too strong with, you know. But the biggest problem was the fact that Kat was never going to forgive him. That couldn't help but mess up the band."

Hazel asked if any of the guys had defended Link's try for Kat. Again Skinny glanced forward before answering and lowered his voice still more, so I could barely hear. He claimed that he and Chris had the most to say about it. Tipsy, as usual, tried to smooth everything over, and Haar was never a guy to make trouble one way or another, even though it was blamed clear he was crazy about Kat.

"What about Watson, where'd he stand?" asked Hazel.

"Hey, he's a piano player, they never stand, they just sit everything out."

"Did anybody ever think maybe the band would be better off without Kat?" I asked.

His eyes opened wide, and I expected his mouth would sag, but instead it tightened up. He shook his head and assured me no one had ever given that a moment's thought.

Hazel asked what he was majoring in at the university. The question seemed to embarrass him, but after a moment he said it was history. He made that sound like a confession.

"Really? Greek, Roman—?"

"American."

"I think that's great. Any special reason?"

Her reaction encouraged him, and his face brightened. "Well, when I started at the U, I didn't have any notion what the heck I wanted to do besides play in a band, but my grandma Tina, who lived with my folks all the time I was in high school, wanted me to get educated and offered to pay my way with money left her by Grandpa, and that seemed better than any jobs handy, so I went. Then at school I had this required history course and the professor was so good I just got all caught up and wanted to go on, so that's what I've decided to do. And even if I wind up never doing anything but playing in a band for a living, it won't hurt one way or another and I'll have had fun."

"When did you learn to play an instrument?" Hazel asked.

He laughed. "Before grade school. Always loved drums—Dad was a drummer with the American Legion band in our town and taught me how to handle the sticks when I was just a little shaver. In high school I got the music teacher to let me work on the traps, and I went nuts. Never had any choice after that—I loved it from the start."

When we got to the edge of South St. Paul and had to slow down, Kat stirred, looked around, and asked Skinny if he'd ever heard Link talk about his father. That got a headshake.

"He talked about him some to me," she said. "The same night he tried to force me. I mean, before we got to my room. He claimed his dad was a big attorney in town, made lots of money and had all sorts of connections with politicians, not just in South St. Paul, but at the capitol. It got really weird. Listening to him when we started walking, I'd have thought his father was his idol, but by the time we got to the apartment building, it was plain he hated him. When I think about it, I realize poor Link didn't really like anybody."

"Except you."

"Oh no, *like* had nothing to do with it. No, he just wanted to use me. Doing it to me would make him feel all bigger, stronger, and superior. That's all he wanted. He hated not being tall."

"How'd you manage to stop him?" I asked.

"I told him if he didn't stop I'd scratch his eyes out."

At that point we pulled up in front of the boardinghouse that Skinny had arranged for us to stay in. As we got out, Chris came around and stood by us. Hazel asked if he thought Link had ever wanted to be leader of the band.

"No. He wasn't a guy who could handle dealing with dance hall owners, or act like a big daddy to a bunch of characters like you find in most bands. He was good enough on his horn to know he could always make out and even stand out, but he wasn't a guy for responsibilities and details."

"How about shortcuts? He strong on those?"

"Well, him trying to force Kat sort of gives you that idea, doesn't it? I've got to say that didn't surprise me any. Actually I feel pretty bad that I didn't warn him not to get too pushy with her. Of course it wouldn't have made any difference, so I don't know why I even think about that."

Kat and Chris made it clear, before dropping us off at a motel a few blocks away from the church where the funeral would take place the next morning at eleven, that they had their own plans for the evening. Hazel decided we ought to see a movie and forget the whole Link mess until the following day. She asked Skinny if he'd like to come with us—we were going to take in a musical that he'd probably enjoy—and to my surprise he said why not?

As we were walking to the theater, we talked some about Kat and her fight with Link. Hazel said, from what we'd heard, it didn't seem like just talk would have stopped Link's assault.

Skinny grinned and said no, it wouldn't have. What really happened was, she rammed her knee between his legs. That stopped him cold.

"Uh-huh," said Hazel, "that would take the starch out. But how come she didn't tell us that?"

"Oh, Kat's a lady, you know. She wouldn't want anybody to know she'd really get that rough."

"She didn't maybe find out in the morning that he bragged the night before to one of you guys that he'd made love to her?"

He stared at her. "Where'd you get that idea?"

"Kat told us," Hazel said.

"Who'd she say told her?" he demanded.

"What difference does it make?"

He was too flustered to find an answer, and then we were at the movie and the whole business was dropped

I don't remember anything about the show. All the time I was thinking about Kat and Link and how much I could believe of anything told me by any of the Kat Klan. My biggest hang-up, of course, was that I didn't want any one of them to take the rap for Link's death. He wasn't the kind of guy who was any great loss, and I couldn't get worked up about the pursuit of justice for its own sake.

In bed that night I told Hazel my feelings. She said that was understandable, but it was plain she wasn't satisfied with the notion of dropping the whole business. Then we got involved in action that didn't call for a lot of chatter, and when it was over, we slept.

20

The funeral was no better or worse than most I've gone to, and there have been all too many of them. It is not a time when a preacher or priest has any freedom to show a sense of humor—most can't even demonstrate a sense of proportion— but this Lutheran kept it brief and made no claims for the saintliness or salvation of the young victim. Mostly he talked about man's inhumanity to man and the sad brevity of Francis Linklater's life. He didn't even mention that the guy had been an exceptional horn man, an omission that several of the band members resented audibly after the service.

I half expected to see Gideon Pryke in the crowd, but he didn't show. Ronald Rochman, however, was standing in the back when Hazel and I got up to leave.

Linklater's mother, at his father's side as they trailed the coffin out, looked as miserable as you might expect. Oran looked like a man who knows everybody is watching, and wants to give the right impression. I had a strong notion his real reaction was relief, that he was glad the service was over, and that he'd been liberated by this death of a son who embarrassed and annoyed him by his rejection of his successful father.

After the services at the cemetery we went back to the church and down in the basement for refreshments. Hazel and I were invited to sit at a table with all the band, including Kat, which only surprised me a little. As we sat down with them, Hazel gave me a raised-eyebrow look, but said nothing.

Tipsy told us, at some length, why he believed beer and booze should be served before, during, and after all funerals, since that was the only way to make the services bearable. Nobody disagreed out loud, but I thought Haar looked embarrassed for him. Kat's eyes roamed the room.

Hazel, who was sitting between Haar and me, asked him if he'd ever met Link's mother. He shook his head. As a matter of fact, he said, he'd never met parents of any of the guys in the band. He suspected parents of all this crowd were folks who generally figured that sons who spent nights blowing horns and beating drums in dance halls had abandoned their families, and they either resented it openly or simply pretended to ignore it.

Hazel remarked that she had heard at least two of the guys learned to play their instruments from their mothers or fathers, so why'd these parents be upset if their kids tried to make a little money with their talents?

"Well," he smiled apologetically, "you have to understand that most of our folks are suspicious of anybody that makes money doing something that's fun. They figure you should only play in churches or concert halls for the glory of God. They get all upset over places like dance halls, where boys and girls have their arms around each other most of the time and get too familiar. And they hear that people who go to dances drink a lot, then go out and sit in cars, necking and worse. Our parents are nearly all puritans, and they never let you forget it."

"Are you including Kat's folks?" asked Hazel.

"I guess her parents weren't, but her grandpa is. I'm not too sure about her grandmother. Far as I know, neither of them ever felt like making much of a fuss about anything Kat really wanted to do."

"I can't picture Linklater's dad being a puritan," I said. "How can a lawyer manage that?"

"Oh, it's easy. Oran's a practicing hypocrite. I heard they've got to prove that to pass the bar exam."

"What's your father do?"

His broad face turned mournful. "He was a butcher until he died of scarlet fever when I was in junior high school."

"How'd your mother manage?"

"She's a high school teacher," he said, with pride. "She was that before I was born, got back into it in the fall after Dad died." Haar suddenly grinned, boyishly. "She enjoys teaching so much that sometimes I think it makes her feel guilty. Whenever she tells me about some kid that she's helped, she thinks she has to tell me about others that she never was able to bring around, you know?"

Hazel asked him who invited Carmen to the intermission party for Kat.

"That was Link. He did it to nettle Kat."

"Did it work?"

"Oh, sure. She's a great actress and didn't let on one way or the other, but I could tell it burned her up all right. Kat wants us all to think she's the only girl that counts. Any time one of us gets interested in some other girl, she starts competing."

"I get the impression that making Kat mad was a hobby of Link's," said Hazel. "Like him bragging to one of you guys about going all the way with her that night he took her home."

He looked startled and stared at her. "Where'd you hear that?"

"It's true, isn't it? That's why she went to the police with the rape story."

At that moment everyone started getting up to leave, and without further comment, Haar moved off.

Rochman was waiting in front of the church when we walked out.

"Mr. Pryke'd like to offer you a ride back to Wisconsin," he said. "Wants to talk with you."

"About murder?"

"By golly," he said, "I guess you really are a detective. Ready to go?"

We rode in the shining black Packard back to the motel and checked out, and Rochman drove us to the Radisson Hotel in downtown Minneapolis, where his boss was staying. Hazel, I suspected, was relieved that since we had been to a funeral, I was practically dressed up. Still I kept getting second looks from bellhops and a few old-lady types who didn't have sense enough to just look at her. We took an elevator to the sixth floor and walked down a hall to Pryke's first-class suite, which was a dream parlor Ma would have died to have in the Wilcox Hotel. We sat down and sank halfway to the floor in the softness of a broad, deep blue couch. Rochman hiked to a distant door and after a couple taps, went inside.

"May I suggest," said Hazel softly, as she gazed around, "that whatever Mr. Pryke wants you to do, you agree to take a shot at it?"

"Is it okay if I wait to hear what it is first?"

"That will be just fine. Isn't this a grand room?"

I granted it wasn't too shabby, but said I was a little worried about how we'd manage to climb out of this couch.

"If you can't manage," she said, "I'll roll off and help you."

Gideon Pryke came out of his room, swaying from side to side as he navigated with two canes. He looked smaller than ever but was bright-faced and sharply dressed. He took a long time to reach an easy chair near us, then carefully let himself down into it and beamed, first at Hazel, then at me. He thanked us for coming, said he hoped the funeral had not been too tedious, and asked what our immediate plans were.

I admitted they were not exactly mapped out.

"I understand the mayor of Indeville has hired you to solve the murder of the Linklater fellow."

"More or less. The case doesn't seem to be going anywhere."

"I have the impression that resolving it isn't exactly a great goal in your life. You don't much like what you've learned of the man killed, and there are no obvious suspects beyond his former bandmates, who you do like."

"It sounds like you've been cross-examining my wife."

He grinned. His teeth were, I'm sure, the best that money can buy. "I have my sources. And good help. Frankly, I'm no more concerned with who might have killed Francis Linklater than you are. But I *am* convinced there are good and sound reasons to believe resolving this case might lead to who killed my grandson. *That* is something I am determined to learn all about, and deal with. Ronald has talked with lawmen in Aquatown and Corden who assure us that you have a remarkable record of solving murder cases. I'm willing to pay generously for your time and cover all expenses that might come from a thorough examination of all the facts related to Nate's death. Now, Ronald tells me you've agreed to ride back to Wisconsin with us, and that you've checked out of your motel. So let's go down to the car and get under way. We can discuss details of your compensation and go over the case during the trip back."

I looked at Hazel. She couldn't have looked much happier if she'd been married to a rich and handsome young man.

"Okay," I said, "let's go."

ideon sat in the front seat with his shriveled legs curled up so he could turn sideways and talk to us. He began by offering me one thousand, flat out, for catching the killer of his grandson, and said he would pay for reasonable living expenses for up to the end of the year if I needed it for solving the case.

"I'll add this," he said. "I'll pay you the thousand just to satisfy me who the killer is. If you can prove the case in court, you'll get double. How's that sound?"

I allowed it sounded pretty good.

"The mayor," said Hazel, "will probably be a bit unhappy if he gets the impression Carl has given up on solving the Linklater case. He fixed us up with a car, took care of our expenses in Indeville, and all."

"Leave the mayor and the sheriff to Ronald," said the old man. "We'll take care of all that. And your deal for the car won't change as long as you're working on this case."

I asked about his grandson. How well did he really know him? How did he persuade him to try running a farm when he didn't know crap about anything to do with it?

He gave me a tolerant smile.

"It was his own idea. I never made the mistake with Nate that I did with his father, Quinton. I tried to raise my son to be a banker, thinking he'd take over my career, eventually become a partner, and ultimately succeed me. It was hopeless from the beginning. He was a born wastrel and dreamer. Good times, that's all he cared about. A lot like his mother, as a matter of fact, but I don't want to get off on that. Like her when she was young, he had style and looks, I give him that, but well, I don't want to talk about him. Now, Nate, he was different. An honest, good-hearted, and appreciative boy, right from the beginning. He came to stay with me when he was only five. I was not about to make the mistake I did with his father, trying to make a banker out of him too early. No sir, I encouraged him in any directions he showed the slightest interest in. Hired a nanny to take care of him and keep him away from his grandmother. He liked to read, I bought him books; he thought for a time he wanted to be an artist, I encouraged that, got him a tutor, arranged for his visits to fine museums. He was smart enough to realize early that he had no artistic talent, only good taste, and he gave up the brush and palette. When he learned in his early teens that my father had been a farmer in the old country, he asked about those long-gone days and what farming had meant to my family. I suppose I oversold it all. Somehow, once gone from the old country, I managed to glamorize the past, and it was really quite easy to give Nate the idea that living on a farm could be the perfect life, with wonderfully productive summers and long, leisurely winters. . . ."

It was obvious to me that this banker's father had been a gentleman farmer who never handled a hoe, spade, or plow in his life, and that Gideon had not been near a farm since his forgotten youth.

When we stopped at a station for gas and the old man went

to the rest room, I asked Ronald what had happened to Nate's father.

Ronald shook his head. "He was a real case. Worked in one of the old man's banks. Never was much good, but hung around a couple years, got married to a society gal. They had Nate about six months after the wedding, and six months after that, Quinton took off with a sexy bank clerk and over a hundred grand he lifted from the bank. Nobody knows where he went—I've heard it was England. The old man covered up the theft, never made any attempt to find the damned fool. Took over Nate. The mother went off somewhere, I've never heard any details on that. Probably married again."

"Where'd Nate find Carmen?" asked Hazel.

"In some art school in New York, when he was studying there for a while. Mr. Pryke's never said what she was doing in the big city, but I figure she was an artist's model."

When the old man came back to the car, he seemed to have lost steam, and about fifteen minutes later he was asleep in the front seat. Hazel and I spent the time talking about what we'd heard. She wanted to know more about Gideon's wife but agreed with me it wasn't likely the old man would talk about her, and granted it wouldn't make much difference as far as figuring out what had happened with Nate.

When we were approaching Foxton, Gideon woke, sat up, and peered over the seatback at us.

"One thing I've not mentioned to you. We've made arrangements that will bring the Kat Klan band back together. The owner of the dance hall in Foxton has a son who plays trombone, and he has agreed to work with this band if they come back together in this area to play for a few dances. This could give you access to them as a group once more."

"Where would they stay?"

He grinned, which always made him look almost boyish.

"Well, sir, I thought perhaps if I were to make available sleeping bags, a couple tents, and canoes, we could persuade them to camp out on the river. They could practice there, have a rather fine time. Maybe change their name from the Kat Klan to the River Rats."

"Wouldn't there be a problem," asked Hazel, "with five fellows and one girl on a camping trip?"

"Well, it occurred to me that wouldn't have to be serious if we could arrange for a mature couple along, sort of like chaperones. . . ."

Hazel couldn't help grinning. "You mean, like us?"

"Who else?"

He let us off at the motel we'd stayed in before, after telling us that his man had made reservations for us.

"Well," said Hazel as they drove away, "he does rather take a lot for granted, doesn't he?"

"With the kind of dough he's got and the help he hires, he's got a right to," I said, "but it'll be damned interesting to hear how he works out carrying a piano and traps in a canoe."

"From what we've learned about the man so far, I've a strong hunch he'll find a working solution with no trouble."

e were having breakfast the next morning at the café across from Pop's place when Dewey showed up with his usual grin, like a kid eating devil's food cake. He told us that Pryke's man, Ronald Rochman, had been around the night before, talking with the sheriff and the mayor. As usual, the sheriff wasn't happy, but the mayor was floating. Nothing he liked better than close contact with big money, and he really cottoned to the notion that with the rich banker's help, he might just possibly wind up looking very good at the end of this affair.

That same evening, Dewey and his partner had been moving around to the pool hall, Pop's soda parlor, and the restaurant, trying to get a lead on anyone that might've been hosting a crap game or poker session some six months back. They were even provided with photographs of Francis Linklater, which Ronald had picked up from the dead man's father.

"And guess what? We couldn't find anybody that knew anything about any gambling going on anywhere in town with anyone at all, let alone involving the trombone player."

Further checking, with guys connected to the band that the

sheriff's men had reached so far, indicated none of the young men had any clear notion of where Link could have made his bundle. Chris Christenson claimed he'd never asked where the game took place, just assumed it had been Menomonie.

According to Dewey, when Ronald crowded him a little on this, hinting that he understood they were great buddies, Chris denied it strongly, insisting they had never been really close and only occasionally double-dated. He made a strong point of his aversion to having any girl he was romancing in a car being distracted by action of another couple in the backseat.

"There's another angle to this car thing," I said. "Link's old man told me he bought the car for him. In Eau Claire."

"How come you didn't mention that before?"

"Mostly because I don't believe it. I can't quite figure out why he'd lie about this, but there are a couple angles. One of them is, the guy is all screwed up about his whole relationship with his son. He wants us to think they were practically buddies. I don't believe it. I figure this car deal is a fairy tale he's handed his wife to make her think he'd done something special for their boy, since he's dead and can't deny it."

Dewey said he'd check with cops in Eau Claire and see if they could come up with anything, but since we couldn't even give them a positive identification on the car, it didn't seem likely they'd get anywhere. He also thought it might be a good idea for me to get my cop friends in Minneapolis to talk with Linklater about his claim.

Then Dewey went into the problem of the car's disappearance. Like me, Rochman had suggested during his talk with the sheriff that it had been taken to Eau Claire, or more likely, to the Twin Cities. Particularly if the killer had been one of the guys from the band who lived in that area. But how can you make an intelligent search for a car you can't pinpoint beyond it being an

Olds? Okay, the band members said it was a tan four-door and had no damage any of them ever noticed.

"The other angle," I told Dewey, "is that maybe Link took a day off and went around to check on his girlfriend Carmen's home to see if the grandson of a big banker in New York had a bundle stashed away, found it, and went shopping after knocking the grandson off. This is the banker's theory."

Dewey nodded. "Yeah, the sheriff told me. He thinks it's baloney, at best, but with the big money man pushing it, he figures he's got to play along. So now we've got to hit all of the car dealers around, see if this kid showed up with cash to buy a car."

"Well, they'd be pretty likely to remember the deal, if it went that way. And it might be a good idea, when asking about it, to also ask if a young woman might have done the buying. Or maybe some other young guy."

Dewey grinned at me. "You're thinking maybe the wife, Carmen, might have done it for her lover, or one of the band guys was in with him?"

"It's an angle. And right now, that's about all we've got to work with."

"You got a fine, dirty mind. I like that."

"How do you like Rochman?"

"I don't know him that much."

So he didn't like him. I guessed the attitude of the New York man would have been condescending toward the local sheriff, and he'd more than likely ignore a deputy entirely.

"You think he's smart?" I asked.

"Not as smart as *he* thinks he is."

"So, is this guy busy pulling the band together and setting up dancing deals for them?"

"You got it. It'll take him a few days, so you might as well get back to your honeymooning."

"Has the old man thought about getting Carmen in on this camping thing?"

"It wouldn't surprise me, but I haven't heard anything about it yet. If you're real lucky, Rochman might team up with her and join you for the trip."

azel and I went back to Indeville and had a short conference with the mayor. He suggested I call the Minneapolis police for a talk with Logan. I did, and he told me he'd work through the South St. Paul station for a follow-up on Linklater's tale. He'd report back to the Indeville mayor. With that settled, Hazel and I got our canoe stocked with grub and were all set for more honeymoon holidays.

We shoved off a little before noon on a bright clear day, without enough wind to cause a ripple on the river's dark, mirrored surface. Changes on the St. Croix, when you're paddling with a slow current, are so gradual you seem at times to be motionless. As you round a long bend, an entirely fresh view slowly opens up. A triple-arch steel bridge comes in sight ahead, a deep red cabin appears off to the left, and you get a sudden glimpse of a railroad with telephone poles lining it. Or, for a time, the banks become steep on each side, and the view of the sky seems limited. Then, slowly there's blue everywhere, high above and low at the edges of the leveled horizon.

It took about half an hour's easy paddling to reach the island where we had spent our first river nights, and we decided to stop there for lunch. Goldfinches were flitting all over the lower island, which was covered with willows so dense it was like a miniature jungle, and we saw flocks of song sparrows along the ridge on the west that separated the lake beyond from the mainstream of the St. Croix. Gulls and crows sailed and flapped overhead. There were tiny bright blue-green flying beetles among weeds at the south end of the island, where Hazel tried casting for a while and came up with nothing but little crappies, which she released gently. We lunched on ham sandwiches with radishes, little green onions, and potato chips.

When we had finished eating and were drinking hot coffee, Hazel asked why I had suddenly decided it was safe for us to be on the river again.

"I'm not that sure it is. But I guess I just can't figure any of this band crowd know their way around here well enough to be a real threat. And I don't know anybody else to worry about seriously. How come you didn't ask until now?"

"Because I wanted to come back out here."

A few minutes later she asked how come I had always been a maverick.

"It probably began when I was a little punk, and the kid from the next farm broke my nose with a rock from his slingshot while I was sitting on the barn roof. It made me look like a tough guy, and nobody ever let me forget it."

"You were on top of a barn when you were just a little kid? Somehow that makes me suspect you were wild from the womb."

"Well, it always seemed natural to me to avoid grown-ups. Sometimes that meant going out of my way to manage it."

"You always try to give the impression you're a natural-born bum, but I've seen the way you sweat to paint good signs, and know how aggressive and persistent you've been in hunting down killers, so the pose isn't very convincing. Maybe you've always gone through all the travel thing to prove to your parents they had no hold or influence on you. Just like you kept drifting all your life, to avoid letting anybody have any real hold on you, direct or indirect."

"So, how come I married you?"

"I'm working on that. I think it comes from a natural instinct to go against the grain, even when it's your own. It's like you can't stand for anybody telling you what to do, including Carl Wilcox."

I shook my head. "What made a smart girl like you pick a nut like me to marry?"

"Because I'm almost as independent and contrary as you are, and somehow you're more fun than anybody else I've known. So many guys are too full of themselves, especially when they're able to dominate people with either muscle or brain power. Of course it doesn't hurt that you make me feel like I'm the sexiest woman alive. Some nights I think that could take care of everything."

"Some nights?"

"Most nights. Come on, Carl, nobody hits the bull's-eye every time."

After finishing lunch we briefly discussed staying on the island, but finally decided it might be smarter to move farther downstream, pick a place on the Minnesota side, and make camp in the least conspicuous place we could find.

In less than half an hour we located a relatively high island on the western edge of the river. It was separated from the mainland by a creek a dozen feet wide, and there was a small clearing on the creek side, well hidden from the St. Croix River, where we put up our pup tent and then briefly explored the area. There wasn't a cabin anywhere near that we could find. Eventually we returned to our new island and fixed a simple dinner of hot dogs, potato chips, and little green onions.

When the mosquitoes moved in just before dusk, we cleaned up the dinner stuff and retreated to the tent and its netting.

I woke to the sounds of songbirds and harsh crow calls, got into my duds, and crawled out into the bright morning. Again the water was glassy and the river seemed broader than ever, the distant trees along the banks a brighter green, and the sky pure blue. I gathered kindling, made a small fire, put coffee on, peeled two oranges, and set them on clean green leaves on the sand beside the fire pit. Hazel came out of the tent looking sleepy, shy, and mussed, gave me a wave, and went into the brush south of our camp.

A few minutes later she came back, went into the tent, and soon reappeared, dressed, combed, and thoughtful. She sat down, ate the fruit I'd put out for her, and when she'd finished it, walked down to the beach, rinsed her hands in the dark water, wiped them on her shorts, and came back to frown at me. "Do you think Link and one of the other band men robbed and killed Carmen's husband?"

I shook my head. "Everything we've picked up on him makes him a total loner. If he teamed up with anybody at all, it had to be Carmen. From everything we've heard, Link wasn't a guy who'd recruit anybody from the band to do anything, least of all murder. We just can't get a handle on this bird. If he did kill, I'd guess it was a solo job, probably done when he was pretty well tanked up and figured the time was ripe for him to do Carmen a favor and maybe latch onto a nice bundle. I'm pretty damned sure the old man hadn't given Nate enough money to make the take high enough for two. On top of all that, I've got a little problem picking any of the other band guys doing it. There was just no incentive for any of them to get involved. That makes it look like a solo job."

She thought a moment, then nodded. "From all we've heard,

that makes sense. It's easy to believe a woman like Carmen could inspire him to get rid of her husband for her. I wouldn't put it past her to drop hints to Link that there was a hidden bundle of money around and that her husband was going to be alone that night. It would seem like a sure thing, especially when she had the excuse of her sick father to get her out of town when the murder was committed."

"So why'd somebody kill Link?"

"I'd guess it was something that had nothing to do with Nate's killing. More than likely one of the band members did it because Link had done their dream girl wrong."

"You think Kat might have put them up to it?"

"Well, if she did, I wouldn't be surprised. Kat doesn't strike me as a kitten. She wasn't so much offended by the physical act— it was his treating her like something inferior. *That* she just couldn't tolerate."

Somehow the notion of any of the band members being involved still didn't sing for me, but I decided to let it ride.

My suggestion that we paddle back downstream farther, just exploring, didn't appeal to Hazel. She thought we should stick around the murder scene, maybe even poke around the area a little more, looking for some sort of clue that would be useful. That was okay with me, although I wasn't optimistic about finding anything.

So we broke camp, loaded the canoe, and paddled steadily against the current until we reached the creek that hooked and crooked its way from the lagoon below the steep eastern bank. While we paddled along the water's edge, we saw a blue bunting that stayed frozen and silent in bushes on the bank as we passed, then suddenly flitted off. We were moving toward the narrower southern end of the lagoon when I caught sight of movement in the brush on my right and turned to look.

There was nothing moving in sight, and when I stopped

paddling to look more closely, Hazel twisted around with raised eyebrows and asked what was up.

"Damn if I know—thought something moved over there. Maybe a deer—" She leaned slightly forward and suddenly smiled. "It's a boy."

Then I saw him, watching solemnly from beside a tree just beyond some low brush.

I waved and said hi. He moved around the brush and approached the bank like a cautious but curious cat. Overalls hung from his wiry frame, the pantlegs barely reaching his ankles. He was wearing frayed tennis shoes that looked too big for him. His bright blue eyes, wide apart in his darkly tanned face, took me in with a knowing grin. "I bet you're Carl Wilcox," he said.

"You got me. Who're you?"

"David Olson. My folks live up on the bluff next door to the Bacons."

"How'd you get down here?"

"There's a little path back of our place. I use it a lot. Come down and watch birds and muskrats. Sometimes see beaver. They live on the other side and ride down slides they make on the bank over there."

"So, where'd you hear my name, and how come you tagged me?"

"Because of the guy that got killed. Everybody's been talking about it. How he got thrown down on the tracks and you pulled him off so the train didn't smash him up worse. They say you're like a detective."

I kept studying him, decided he was about thirteen, maybe fourteen, and a cagey one. "How'd you know he was thrown over?" I asked.

"Well, that's what everybody thinks. Either that or he got chased over. It'd be pretty dumb just to jump, wouldn't it?"

"Not if he thought he was gonna get shot. Who told you what happened?"

"Well, everybody's been talking about it. You gonna find out who killed him?"

"I've been working on it some. This is Hazel, my wife. She's helping me."

He glanced at her and grinned shyly when she smiled.

"Did you hear the shot that night?" she asked.

"Uh-huh. And the yell."

"Where were you?"

He looked at the shining river for a moment, then glanced back at her. "Can you keep a secret?"

"Sure. You were outside, weren't you?"

"I was down by the tracks. Sometimes I go there and watch for the train. It doesn't always come, but I watch anyway when I don't feel like staying in bed."

"Why don't you feel like staying in bed?"

He shrugged. "I don't want to sleep as much as my folks say."

"Okay. So you got up and went down near the tracks—did you see the man fall?"

"No. Too many trees and leaves and stuff. But I heard yelling till he hit the tracks. It was real spooky."

"What'd you do?" I asked.

"Went home," he said, and looked at me straight in the eye.

"Did your mom and dad see you come in?"

"Naw. I climb the tree by the porch roof and get into my room from there."

"Did your parents mention hearing the scream to you next morning?"

He shook his head.

"Between the time of the shot and the guy's screaming, did you hear anything else?"

After a moment's thought, he shook his head again.

"Didn't you see anything?"

"No, it was too dark and I was too scared when the guy yelled. I ran for home."

"Have you got any idea how long it was between the scream and the time when the man hit the tracks?"

He said it wasn't long but couldn't get any more specific than that.

Hazel frowned, then asked David how well he knew the people next door. He wasn't sure what she meant by that, and she said she wanted to know if he was ever in their house or if they came to his. He said no, they didn't come to his house, but he'd been to theirs. By the time we took him back to his homeward path we knew he'd obviously been a favorite of the Bacons and had more than once kept company with Kat, who like him loved to explore the path to the river and the area along the shore and had learned the names of nearly all the animals and birds around. No, he hadn't seen her much in the last year. She was too busy or gone off to school. On his birthday she sent a card and wrote a note to him, and when he came to their house just before Christmas she gave him a box of Whitman's chocolates and refused to share them, saying they were all for him.

"If it's okay with you," I said, "I'd like to come up to your house and talk to your folks a little."

He looked accusingly at Hazel. "You said you wouldn't tell on me."

"We won't. Carl just wants to see if your parents heard what happened that night. There'll be nothing said about what you told us you did."

He looked at me. "Honest?"

"Absolutely."

He sighed and said okay, but it wouldn't do any good.

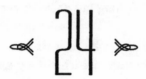

We climbed behind our young guide and were puffing some by the time we reached the top. The long narrow path from the bluff's edge to the Olson house and lot was shaded by oaks, elms, box elders, a few young willows, and a couple cottonwoods.

The house stood on open ground, a white clapboard two-story job, with only a small stoop and two steps up to the screen door in back. Off a ways to the west there was a large shed with double doors. The last part of the walk to the house passed between two broad vegetable gardens filled with corn, potatoes, cabbages, onions, tomatoes, and God knows what else. When we got to the stoop, David pulled the door open, stuck his head inside, and called, "Ma!"

"Don't yell," came a thin voice from inside.

"I got company," said David. He made it sound like a warning.

A second later a small, curly-haired brunette with bright green eyes, a hawkish nose, and a wide mouth appeared in the small vestibule beyond the back door, wearing a blue-and-white apron over a green housedress. Her frown immediately changed at the sight of us to something like fear, then carefully turned into a thin smile as she switched her gaze from me to Hazel and back. She seemed more like a sister than a mother to David.

"Well," she said, "I guess you must be that Wilcox man we've been hearing so much about. I wondered when you'd show up."

"David didn't happen to tell us your name," I said.

"He would've if you asked. He knows it. I'm Ida Olson. My husband's at work. I've got fresh coffee perking, want some?"

"We'd appreciate that," said Hazel.

That got her a grin from Ida. Her teeth were white and even, with a slight gap in the center. She moved to the counter, got cups down for the three of us, not bothering with saucers, took a cream pitcher from the icebox and a sugar bowl from the counter, and set them on the table.

"So," she said, "what do you expect from me?"

"You're neighbors of the Bacons," I said, "so we wondered if anybody from the sheriff's office has talked with you or your husband about the death on the tracks."

"My husband's name is Gunnar. And yes, the sheriff talked with him at the bakery where he works. No policemen have come to talk with me. Why would they?"

"To see if you knew anything helpful. Like whether you heard anything the night the man went over the cliff, since it was right next door to you."

"They're next door, but it's not that close."

"Come on, it was close enough to hear a shot and a yell like the one he made."

She shrugged and said okay, that was Sunday night, wasn't it?

"More like early Monday morning."

"Oh, yes. No, we were sleeping. We both sleep hard. My husband's up and off to work before dawn."

"It was about four when the man went over," I said.

"Oh?" She looked innocent as a newborn babe as she moved to the stove, where the percolator was going full steam by then. We all watched the water turn dark as it hit the glass top and fell back on the grounds.

"Do you see much of the Bacons?" I asked.

"No, not really. You can see our houses are pretty far apart, and we don't visit much. Gunnar's working hours kind of set us apart from most folks."

"You belong to the same church?" asked Hazel.

Ida looked at her directly for the first time since we'd come in. "No, we don't. I heard you two were honeymooning on the river. You really like that?"

"Yes," said Hazel, smiling. "It's very pretty, and wonderfully private."

"So—how'd you two meet?"

"She was the school librarian," I said, "in a jerkwater South Dakota town where I got involved in trying to figure out who murdered a high school student. She turned out to be so helpful I married her. Where'd you hear about me?"

"Well, most of what I know I got from Gunnar. He heard people talking at the bakery. Like you're working for that banker from the East, the grandpa of the man murdered a while back over in Foxton."

The small-town grapevine has newspapers and radio beat all to hell when it comes to passing local stories.

"What do they say in the bakery about the murder here?"

"Oh my, all sorts of things. You wouldn't want to hear some of them."

"Like what?"

"Well, like maybe you had something to do with it—got his car maybe—"

She offered that as though expecting to jolt the hell out of me.

"Do any of them think the sheriff buys that idea?" I asked.

She waved both hands casually, went over to the stove, moved the percolator off the gas jet, and closed down the gas. "Others," she said, "think maybe one of the band fellows did it. And one or two even think it mighta been Kat. You know she learned wrestling from her brother? She knows how to throw a man over her shoulder. David's seen her do it."

"To who?"

"Her brother."

I asked how well she knew Barry. She said pretty well—after all, he worked at the bakery with her husband. Had been there for over three years. That got me thinking more about the timing of Link's fall and the working hours of Ida's husband. It seemed like it might be a good idea to visit the bakery, get some idea of when the boss showed up and how many people would know if the help was around at that hour that particular Monday morning.

But then Gunnar Olson came in.

He wasn't hairy enough to really look like a gorilla, but he had arms and shoulders like one, hunched about the same way, and his eyebrows and scowl were apelike. He was deeply tanned, and it occurred to me he must be the guy who took care of that whopping garden out back. I guessed he was near twenty years older than his wife.

Ida introduced us, and he did little more than grunt before getting his cup of coffee and taking a place at the table across from Hazel and me.

Ida told him what we'd been talking about, and all the while he watched me with eyes that were all Scandinavian blue under the beetled brows.

"Your wife says you start work at four in the morning," I said. He nodded.

"You get up at three?"

"About."

"The Monday morning the guy went over the bluff here—did you hear a shot, or him yell?"

He shook his head and took a drink of coffee. His thin hair was a dark red, and the beginning stubble on his chin made me imagine him as a red-bearded Viking pirate.

"Like I told the sheriff, I was downtown by the time that happened," he said.

"How do you know?"

"Because the train engineer says it was something like four-thirty when he spotted you on the track."

"You talked with him?"

"No, that's just what Barry Bacon heard from somebody. Probably one of the deputies."

"Dewey?"

"Yeah, he's Barry's old school buddy."

"Was Barry at work with you by four?"

"Sure," he said, nodding emphatically and a little too quickly.

"Anybody else at the bakery then?"

No, it had been just the two of them.

I asked how well he knew Kat Bacon, and he said probably as well as his son. She'd been big-sistering David practically from when he was born. He admitted she had become scarce around their place in the past year, but she still kept in touch, like on holidays and any time she got back to town. She sent postcards sometimes and brought presents to David on Christmas and his birthday.

"Got any ideas on who might've killed this Linklater guy?" I asked.

"Probably somebody that wanted to swipe his stash."

"You don't think it had anything to do with Kat Bacon?"

"You mean because he tried to screw her this spring? Naw. None of them hornblowers and such'd have the balls for that."

"I hear she got wrestling lessons from her brother, Barry. Maybe she did it herself."

"Nah. If she'd done it, she'd admit it. Just say he tried her again and she fought him and he fell."

"What would you have done if you caught that guy trying to rape her?"

"I wouldn't have just thrown him down on the tracks. I'd have pitched him clear to the goddamn river."

"You go out and look at your garden before you take off for the bakery?"

"Nah, just walk straight into town."

"That takes you past the Bacon place."

"Not through their backyard."

"You see a car by their house?"

"Never looked. They got parking space behind it—if the car was back there, I couldn't have seen it if I'd tried."

From what I'd seen of the area, it wasn't hard to believe him, but the timing was hard to ignore.

After a few more minutes of talk that went nowhere, we left.

azel suggested we drift over past the Bacon place. We strolled along the wooded area dividing the lots and once more looked around where Link's flight had probably begun. It was well beyond the view of anyone in either the Olson or Bacon houses. There was no way Gunnar could have seen Link accidentally from the road. On the other hand, it was most likely that Link had been on the road, maybe parked his car there, and Gunnar could have sighted him moving toward his house, or even intercepted him.

When I mentioned this to Hazel, she shook her head. We had no reason to believe Gunnar knew anything about the guy, she said, and he struck her as the last person in the world who would fall in love with a car enough to kill its owner and take it over—especially when he wouldn't ever dare use the car.

"Maybe so," I granted, "but you've got to remember, Kat's brother works with Gunnar. If they've become buddies, then what'd be more natural than for them to pair up and settle this horntooter's hash once and for all? Both of these guys are strong, we know Barry's into wrestling, and I'm positive he's protective as hell about his sweet sister. If Link made the mistake of trying to pull something with Kat at around four in the morning, those birds would be just the ones to put the kibosh on him."

"I just can't quite imagine her being up and around at that hour. Of course," she said, frowning thoughtfully, "maybe she'd had a little get-together with one of the other band guys. If Link somehow got wise to that, he might have hung around to catch her coming home."

Talking about it further, we both had a problem believing Link would have been dumb enough to make another pass at Kat at her home. Unless, as Hazel suggested, he was stupid drunk, or for some reason had been lured there.

I decided to stop by the sheriff's office and check if there'd been any word from the St. Paul police about their interview with Link's lawyer father. Steiger said there'd been no call. We finally gave the whole business up for the time, walked back to our canoe, and paddled to the island where we'd been camping when all this business began. The reason was simple; it was handy to a fresh water supply from the spring on the bank, it was within easy reach of a decent-sized lake to the west, and the views of the river from the island were broad and open, with no houses or even chimneys in sight, yet we could reach civilization in less than an hour if we needed to. We would also have a good view of any traffic on the river. When Hazel asked how come I'd stopped worrying about getting attacked, I told her it seemed unlikely anybody around figured we were any kind of threat, the way things had gone so far.

"I suppose there's something to that," she granted, "but I suspect the real reason is, you'd like to take this party on in our territory."

I didn't try to argue the point.

A little after ten on Thursday morning Hazel and I were

fishing off the lower end of the island when we heard a motor upstream. I put down my pole and ambled north through the thin woods to the small beach at the head of the island. Well upstream, a large raft on pontoons was moving slowly down the river toward us. Gradually I made out six figures, five guys and a girl.

I went quickly back to Hazel and called to tell her we were about to have visitors. Her eyebrows went up, but she accepted my word, pulled in her line, and walked back to the point at my side.

"Well," said Hazel, taking in the approaching band, "I told you the old man would figure out how to handle a piano and traps on the river."

Tipsy, Dutch Haar, and Kat were all up front. Beyond them was Chris, handling the outboard motor on the stern. Nolan Watson was leaning one elbow on an upright piano, and Skinny Engen, nearby, perched on the rail looking forward. All of them were grinning except Kat. She just looked thoughtful.

As the pontoons plowed into the shallows of the point and scraped on the sand, Tipsy tossed us a salute and announced that they'd been sent by their godfather, Gideon Pryke, to be our personal band for the rest of our honeymoon.

"We heard the old man was lining up some jobs for you," said Hazel, "but he didn't say you were going to do them on a raft."

"We won't, this is just our portable rehearsal hall," said Tipsy, as Dutch Haar and Chris jumped ashore, both hanging on to lines attached to the pontoon fronts, and began pulling the craft up tight.

"When's your first job?" I asked.

"Next Saturday night we're doing it in the Hudson dance hall," said Tipsy.

"Well, you'll have to find another island for camping. This one's not big enough to handle all of you."

"Okay, Dad, don't panic, we'll just leave the Kat with you. We understand you old folks'll be her chaperone through the dark nights. Know a good spot nearby for us?"

I suggested they go west across the river to the islands separating the lake beyond from the mainstream. Tipsy looked about with vague interest, while Chris stared across the smooth, shining water to the green banks beyond and the bluffs back and high above, lined by trees and brush along the ridge.

"Oh," said Tipsy, "I'm supposed to tell you, the St. Paul police talked with Link's old man a day or so ago. They told the sheriff that Linklater claimed he'd actually not gone with his son to buy the car—just gave him cash and let him handle the buying on his own. He doesn't know who he bought it from—whether it was a used car lot or from the former owner."

That sounded like baloney to me, but I thanked Tipsy for passing the message and figured I'd have to get further into that business.

The band decided the first thing to do was run a rehearsal before lunch. A short one. So they gathered on the pontoon raft, which tilted slightly on the sandy slope, and went through a couple numbers. I wondered, while listening to them and watching, if they missed Link's trombone and person, but all I know is, they sounded fine, maybe even good. It seemed like all of their blowing and pounding would cause echoes along the river valley, but none came back to us, and it was as though the band silenced the birds and even the insects.

We had lunch together. They had brought ham and brown bread, so we made big sandwiches with mustard, gobbled potato chips, and drank Leinenkugel beer carried in a big cooler and stacked around a solid chunk of ice in its center.

Hazel asked where their new trombonist was, and Tipsy said he couldn't join them until their first job, but they'd manage.

"Level with us," Chris said as we were picking up the paper plates and tossing them onto the shallow fire pit for burning later. "Was as it your idea to get us out here with you?"

"It was not," said Hazel. "All we volunteered to the banker was, we'd put up Kat if she was willing, and we'd talk and listen with you guys and her."

"You really think one of us did him in?" asked Dutch.

"It's just one of the possibilities we've got to think about," I said. "Right now it's pretty hard to swallow that idea, even if Kat was mad enough to want him dead. It seems a lot more likely he got killed because of what happened to Nate Pryke."

Kat's eyes opened wide. "You think Carmen had something to do with it, right?"

"It's one angle."

"I don't get it," said Tipsy. "Why'd she want to knock off anybody for doing her hubby in, when she probably wanted to get rid of him anyway?"

"Maybe because the killer took all of her husband's stash and bought a car for himself. Or maybe she got crazy jealous when she found out Link had been drooling after Kat."

I asked if they'd mind telling exactly what each of them had done Sunday night, where they had been, and what witnesses they had to prove they couldn't have been around the Bacon farm.

Kat, with what I took to be a touch of sweet sarcasm, said she'd been in bed at her grandparents' place, and couldn't claim that either one of them watched her sleep all night.

Dutch Haar, Nolan Watson, and Tipsy Tobler claimed they had all driven in Tobler's car to the Twin Cities. Chris said he had driven Skinny Engen to Menomonie and then went on home to Chippewa Falls. They all agreed it was about nine-thirty when their river party broke up. The trip to the Twin Cities from Indeville was roughly two hours. It would take about three hours from there to Menomonie. It was about six hours from the party breakup time until Link went over the cliff—time enough for either Chris or Skinny to make a trip back to the killing. It was even time enough for Dutch, Nolan, or Tipsy to come back for the job. And of course, if either the pair or the trio went directly to the Bacon farm, they had plenty of time to handle Link's trip to the tracks.

Somehow none of these alternatives seemed likely to me. And then there was the question of when Kat meandered back home. She had a lot of unaccounted-for time. I figured I'd get back to that later. "Why do you guys figure old Gideon is spending his dough to give you a river trip and special jobs?" I asked.

"Haven't you got that figured out?" asked Chris.

"Maybe. But I'd like to know what you guys think."

"We've talked it over," said Tipsy. "The best we've come up with is, he hopes you can get buddy-buddy with us and work out how to make a case for Link being the guy who killed his nephew. We figure he's got a notion, or at least hopes, that one or more of us was in on it, and thinks if you work on us enough, you can nail whoever did it."

"So how come you decided to go along with him?" .

"Well, hell, if we said no, it'd just make him more suspicious, and a guy who's loaded with dough like this guy's got, he could give us a lot of trouble. We know damned well there's no case you can make against any of us, so we go along, get a nice vacation, and on top of that, we get two or three dance jobs we wouldn't have had otherwise. How can we lose?"

"Didn't anybody argue against it?" I asked, looking them over.

"Not a one," said Tipsy, and gave me a smug grin.

Hazel looked at Kat, who'd taken all of this in without a flicker of expression. "Do you think Link could have killed Nate Pryke?" she asked.

Kat frowned. I thought she wanted to look sad, but actually her expression was almost grim. "I don't know. I'm afraid I never did begin to understand Link. He was the best musician I've ever known personally, yet he was very unsure of himself most of the time, at least when he was sober. The night he walked me home, he told me how his father was against him and his mother was weird and he had always been lonely and even the fellows in the band were really strangers. At first I felt real sorry for him, but when I hugged him he suddenly turned into an animal, pawing me and trying to get me down on the couch. He seemed to become another person. I couldn't believe it. I was surprised how strong he seemed, and panicked. Later, after he was gone, I kept thinking about it all and couldn't make sense of it. After the way he changed in seconds, I could believe almost anything about him. Even the business of killing Carmen's husband. If he did do it and got any help, I'd say it had to be from Carmen, but I don't think he'd have let her know what he had in mind—he wouldn't think she was smart enough to be any real help if she understood what he was up to."

The guys seemed to agree with that—at least, none of them contradicted or challenged her—and the subject died.

After the guys took off to set up their own camp, Hazel asked Kat if she would rather have a pup tent of her own instead of sharing our pyramidal. She shook her head. "Staying alone in one of those things would give me the creeps. I'd rather share with you two, if you don't mind."

The fact was, I minded plenty, but Hazel assured her it would be just fine, and the two of them went inside with Kat's bedroll and overnight bag to get organized. I figured Hazel would set things up so she'd be between our visitor and me.

Suddenly our island was no longer private and exclusive.

decided to get a supply of water from the spring on the eastern bank, went down, climbed into the canoe, and paddled over. A footstep on crackling twigs jerked my head up as I was kneeling over the sparkling spring water; less than six feet away, David Olson stood watching me.

He nodded at my greeting and walked slowly forward in fairly new blue jeans, a blue shirt with the sleeves rolled up, and moccasins. His expression was less wary than at our first meeting. He carried a long bamboo fishing pole and maneuvered it carefully through the brush.

"What kind of bait you use?" I asked.

"Grasshoppers."

After filling my water jug and putting it back in the canoe, I told him I had another question to ask. He only looked a little apprehensive as he met my eyes.

"I've got a real problem," I told him, "accepting the idea that when you heard the man go over the cliff, you didn't go around to see what happened. I just can't figure you as a guy who'd turn chicken. It seems more likely you went to the tracks, found him, couldn't tell who he was because the face was smashed, so you dug out his wallet to find his name."

He kept meeting my stare and didn't blink. Finally he took a deep breath and glanced toward the river, then back at me.

"What difference would it make if I did?"

"None at all if you'd put the wallet back. Why didn't you?"

"I heard somebody coming up the hill. It scared me and I just took off, carrying it with me."

"So you found out who he was. Did you tell Kat?"

"I didn't tell anybody." He didn't meet my eyes when he said that, but then he looked up. "It wasn't like I stole it. I mean, it was no good to him anymore—"

"How much money was in it?"

"Twenty-two dollars."

"Where's the wallet now?"

"I dumped it in our garbage. Are you going to tell on me?"

"I won't tell your old man, maybe not anybody else if I can help it. Now, is there anything else you want to tell me about this whole business?"

He shook his head.

"Okay, don't worry about it. Now I'm going to take you over to the island. We've got a friend of yours with us."

He looked skeptical. "Who?"

"Come along and find out."

After a second's deep thought, he nodded and followed me to the canoe. He asked if he could use the paddle in the bow and grinned when I said feel free. After bumping the canoe side once, he adjusted enough to avoid any repetition of that by leaning to his right.

"Just take it easy," I told him. "You don't really have to work a canoe paddle hard unless you're bucking a current."

We covered the few yards to the island, and he rested the

paddle across his knees as I guided us up on the sand, slipped his moccasins off, and hopped into the shallow water, barely getting his jean ends wet as he pulled the bow up. I told him he was a natural, and he may have blushed, but it was hard to tell with all that tan.

Before he turned around, Kat, who had just emerged from the tent, saw who was with me and yelled, "David!"

He turned with a jerk and stumbled in the sand, his face glowing as he started toward her. It was plain he wanted to run, but he managed to walk with some dignity as she ran to meet him. He got a whopping hug and a warm kiss on the cheek before his arms came up to hug her back.

I carried the water to a shady spot by the tent, and Hazel moved over beside me as the young pair talked excitedly—or at least, Kat did. David was practically tongue-tied for several seconds. After the embrace they had separated a little awkwardly, then slowly she led him toward the beach, a ways beyond us.

"Did he know she was here?" Hazel asked me.

I shrugged and said just maybe.

She watched them, frowning thoughtfully, before turning to me again. "I can't believe there wasn't some special reason he was out and around when Link went over that bluff. Kids are always trying to stay up later than their parents, but I've never known one in my life who wanted to get up ahead of them—especially when the father regularly got up at three. That's too much to swallow."

"Okay, so what've you figured got him up?"

"Maybe he knew Kat was around. Maybe in the past they got together at weird hours, like after she'd been at a dance, or some other sort of high school thing, like a play. Maybe she even sang for a band back when she was in high school—we don't know. . . ."

"It sounds like you've got them being lovers. Come on, Hazel, he must be at least five or six years younger than she is—"

"I'm not saying they've been making love. Kids can get involved with each other without going all the way, and I think Kat's a very affectionate and needing girl who can't get enough attention. Maybe it's something caused by her father discouraging greater closeness between her and her brother. From everything we've seen and heard, she just has to have every male she meets crazy about her."

"I haven't noticed her cozying up to me."

"Well, you may be young at heart, but you're almost old enough to be her daddy, so I suppose she sees you as being on the other side. Wait till we've shared the island and a tent a couple nights. Maybe she'll change her attitude. But don't get any ideas. I'm a very light sleeper."

"I don't know. If we have to spend up to a week with a third party in the tent, my ideas might go beyond the moon, but I could be all taken care of by a little walk in the woods a couple times a day. Just you and me."

She turned thoughtful and finally shook her head. "I've got a better idea. Whenever they're in rehearsal, we'll just take her over to their island and leave her until they finish. Then we wouldn't have to walk any farther than the tent once we paddled back here. And if we skip going to whatever dances they play for, we'll have lots of solo time."

"For a romantic type, you've got to be the most practical woman I've ever met. I mean, you get all the priorities worked out toot sweet. How about we grab a quickie while the kids are gabbing?"

"No thanks, quickies aren't my style. What we should work on right now is how come David was up when he was on the night of the murder, and whether he'd been with Kat before it happened."

I grinned and accepted her suggestion that we amble over

and see if we could learn anything from the young ones, who were sitting side by side on the riverbank. On the way I told her what I'd learned from David about what happened to Link's wallet. Before she had time to probe me on that, Kat saw us out of the corner of her eye as we approached and said something to her partner.

"Well," said Hazel when we were next to them, "how about the four of us take a canoe ride? Carl and I can paddle, and you two talk."

Kat looked at David, who stared back at her soberly.

"All right," said Kat, after a second, "let's go."

They sat side by side, with their backs to me. She tilted her head his way, and most of what I could hear was about the band's many jobs in the Twin Cities area and a couple in Wisconsin quite recently and what great reactions they got when she sang. Soon she tried to get him talking, but he was self-conscious with Hazel and me so near and only mumbled a bit in response to questions she asked about school. He finally told her a little about his scout camp time.

We pulled up to a small island I wanted to check out. While we wandered as a group, I spotted a muskrat hustling into the water ahead of us, clutching a clump of brush in his jaws. When he had paddled out of sight along the island bank, Hazel casually asked David how in the world he'd happened to be awake before four A.M. the night the man went over the cliff.

He hemmed and hawed until Kat suddenly told him to go ahead and tell what had happened—it'd have to come out some time.

He finally told us he'd gotten up and gone out because he heard his parents yelling at each other. He was afraid there was going to be a fight like there'd been before, and he couldn't stand to listen. He wasn't sure of the time—he didn't have a clock in his room—but it was going on when his father was having break-fast, which would make it a little after three-thirty. I asked if his dad ever hit his mother, and he said no in a tone that suggested he thought I was nuts to even think of it.

He said he hadn't seen anybody around the house when he crawled out the window, climbed down the tree, and went directly to the river path. Yes, he'd known Kat was home, but figured she'd be in bed and never considered wandering over by the house after bedtime. I watched Kat eyeing David, and her expression made me wonder. There was too much approval evident.

We got nothing more from them, and finally we went back to our island.

e had only been back a few moments when we heard
Gunnar on the nearby shore, calling for David. I got the
boy in the canoe, and we paddled over to meet his father,
who stood on the grassy bank, scowling at us all the way. He
scolded David for worrying his mother and wanted to know
where the hell he'd been, while pointedly ignoring me. I told him
where we'd been and that Kat had gone with us. My explanation
didn't improve Gunnar's mood. At the mention of Kat he
clouded up more than ever and glared at his son.

"Has this guy been asking you questions about your family?"
he growled.

"He only wanted to know did I see anybody in back of the
Bacons' place the night the guy got killed."

"How the hell'd you see anybody from your room?"

"That's what I told him—that I couldn't."

Gunnar looked suspicious of that answer, but I figured he
didn't have the imagination to think that his kid would ever climb
out the window of his room and shinny down a tree to go exploring on his own.

"I was wondering," I said, "has Barry ever talked to you any about his sister and the guy Linklater who tried to rape her this spring?"

"What's it to you?"

"I just want to know how mad that made him."

"What the hell'd you think? It made him mad as hell. But that don't mean he pitched him off the cliff. Him and me were going to work when that business happened."

"The timing was pretty handy."

His scowl got meaner. "You think you can pin that business on us?"

"I'll tell you a little secret, Gunnar, I don't really give a damn who killed Linklater. What I'm after is who killed Nate Pryke. It seems likely it was Linklater, and that's all I really want to prove. If you can give me any help in nailing that, it'll take the heat off finding Link's killer."

"That's because Nate's rich grandpa'll pay you to nail somebody for that one, right?"

"You've got that straight. But it's still a fact that Nate, from all I've heard, was generally a guy nobody had any good reason to kill. Link was maybe something else, but I'm not sure what."

"Well, I didn't see anybody kill either one of these guys, so just forget about me and Barry. Come on, David, your ma's waitin' supper."

David gave me an apologetic nod, and they left.

Back on the island I asked Kat how she got on with Gunnar. She shrugged and made her mouth droop. "He's always been fairly civil to me, but it bothers him that David likes me better than him. He's just a born grump. It really doesn't mean much. The trouble is, he's always hollering at Ida, which gets David so upset he runs off and wanders around the railroad tracks and the riverbank. He can't bear their fussing at each other."

"How do you get along with Ida?"

"Just fine. She can be kind of a nut, but she's got a big heart."

Hazel smiled. "How does she react to Gunnar's hollering?"

"Oh, she hollers back. Tells him, 'I ain't afraid of you, Gunnar Olson!' And she's not. He never hits her."

I figured that was lucky. If he did, he would probably knock her through a wall.

"Does he hit David?" I asked.

"Well, I think he's cuffed him a few times, but never enough to leave a mark. Gunnar's not as bad as he looks." She laughed. "Hardly anybody could be."

"Has he ever hollered at you?" asked Hazel.

"No. He's sort of growled a few times, but back when I was around a lot, I made a point of staying out of his sight as much as possible. I know he kept telling David he should hang around with fellas and quit cozying up to his nursemaid—which is what he called me, trying to shame him."

Hazel asked Kat if any of the band had ever met the Olsons. She said yes, Ida had come around to one of their Wednesday-night dances during Easter vacation, and brought David to see and hear her singing with the band. The three of them spent an intermission in a booth at a restaurant next door, and Ida wanted to know all about what it was like, working with and getting to know all these guys in the band and meeting all sorts of other guys who came to the dances and fell for her. I gathered that Kat was unloading good when Link dropped by and moved in. Right away, all of Ida's attention switched to the guy, and of course Link just loved that and encouraged her shamefully.

"You think they got together later?" I asked.

"Well, she sure did everything she could to encourage him, and I'll admit I was a little surprised he got interested so quick. For heaven's sake, Ida was a good ten years older than he was, maybe more. Not that Link wouldn't go for older women—he'd go for anything in a skirt—or out of it, for that matter—if she paid him the least attention. But after all, she had David with her, so how could they have worked anything out?"

Kat said the four of them had walked back to the dance, and she couldn't remember any time when Ida and Link had a chance to set up a meeting, although, when she thought about it, she recalled seeing Ida and Link later, having a short chat by the bandstand before they split. They probably could have made some agreement on where and when to get together then, because David was busy talking with Kat. The more Kat thought about that, the surer she was that something had been worked out between the couple. She remembered Link looking very smug as he took up his trombone for the first number when they resumed playing.

I asked if Ida and David had stayed around until the end of the dance. She said no, they'd gone home shortly after the intermission. Kat couldn't remember seeing Link after the dance. She had been given a ride to her parents' place for the night by Tipsy.

Hazel offered Kat a fish dinner. She said gee, she'd like that, but the fellows had planned on her joining them for steaks and would be around to pick her up pretty soon. Then they'd have another practice session and bring her back to our island later.

I suggested it'd be simpler for us to give her a ride over, and that's what we did. The guys invited us to stay, they had plenty of food for all, and we agreed. It didn't come as any surprise that they never mentioned the murders we were concerned about. All the talk was of the band, what they would play Saturday night, the sort of crowd they expected, and some reminiscing about past jobs they'd done and dancers they'd enjoyed. It was all innocent as kindergarten and about as useful to Hazel and me, although we both enjoyed the steaks, onions, and baked potatoes provided.

And of course there was beer. I tried to corral Tipsy to ask some questions, but he put me off.

It was near midnight when we paddled back to the island with Kat. Hazel suggested that she and I take a little walk to the south end of the island while our guest got ready for bed, and we admired a half-moon that seemed to be almost framing a bright star off to the southwest.

"What's your opinion of Kat's story about Link getting interested in Ida?" Hazel asked.

"I think she dressed it up some when she claimed she saw the two of them talking by the bandstand while David was gabbing with her."

"Uh-huh. That's just what I thought."

My suggestion that she go back and get a blanket so we could have a cozy round before bed didn't go over. So after some kidding we went back to the silent tent and got in our separate sacks. If Kat was still awake, she didn't let us know.

I heard movement beyond Hazel's sleeping bag in the morning and opened my eyes, but it was still dark enough inside so I couldn't make out what was going on. Then I was wide awake and saw Kat slipping out through the tent flap. She moved into the dim light and her pajamas became visible, pink and snug around her perfectly curved bottom. When I turned toward Hazel, I saw her head lifted, watching me.

"Pretty neat, huh?" she said.

"Almost as good as yours," I admitted.

Hazel pushed down the sleeping bag and crawled out. She was wearing her underpants and bra, and it was only seconds before she'd pulled them off, slipped into her swimming suit and moccasins, and moved outside. I got up, pulled on my trunks, and followed.

Hazel had moved down to the beach by the time I got out. The sun wasn't quite up, but the eastern sky was all aglow and the smooth river sparkled brilliantly, reflecting all its glory. Kat was nowhere in sight. I moved out beside Hazel.

"Where'd she go?" I asked.

"I think she's doing her morning thing in the woods, just as

I will when she gets back. You want to take a morning dip before breakfast?"

It seemed warm enough, and since I didn't figure it would be smart to wander the woods picking up kindling while Kat was probably somewhere in a squat, I agreed to hit the water, and in we went.

We made it brief, but by the time we came out, Kat was back, had slipped into whoopee pants and a shirt, and was digging through our cooler looking for breakfast fruit. We joined her and all peeled our own oranges and ate the sections as the sun came in sight, turning the banks bright green, the sky pale blue, and the river a mirror for it all. Then, while I made a fire and Hazel filled the coffeepot with water and measured coffee into the filter, we started talking.

Hazel asked Kat how she'd slept, and she said not long after midnight she woke and couldn't get back to sleep. "I just kept going over everything and couldn't stop worrying. I feel sure you suspect me of being responsible, one way or another, for Link's death. I keep thinking, how can I convince you I didn't have anything to do with it? Because it was *not* me. I didn't even trick him into coming around so one or more of the fellas could throw him over. None of us felt what he did was all *that* bad. I didn't want anything to do with him, but I certainly didn't have to have him killed to keep him off. I'll admit, I was bitter at first about him treating me like a tramp and bragging to the band that he'd made me. That's what made me start to bring charges against him, but I'm not crazy enough to think that calls for murder. Can you believe I'm that kind of a maniac?"

I got a loaf out of our breadbox and set up things for toasting it as soon as we could get the scrambled eggs started, while I worked on my answer. "Let me try out a few notions that have come by me the last few days. We got the fact that Link died practically in your backyard. There's no question about that. Why? He sure as hell didn't come around there to admire the view of the river or even try a high dive. So what other reason would he have for being in your neighborhood? You think it's impossible that he was so hot for you he simply couldn't give up? What if he thought there was a chance he'd find you wandering because somewhere along the line, back when you and he were getting on okay, you told him about what things were like around your grandparents' place? Maybe you even told him you went for walks at wild hours, because you liked the view—or maybe because, now and then, you met your young friend David, who had a habit of ducking out on his parents' fights and exploring the territory at weird hours."

She stared at me a second before managing a smile. "You've been talking with David, haven't you? So yes, that's how we really became friends. It happened after I'd done my first job with a dance band and got home real late and still wasn't sleepy because I was all fired up by the evening, which had been real special, with a big crowd and lots of guys and even girls coming around to say how much they liked my singing. I walked out in back of the house to look at the river and saw David, wandering way down there by the tracks. He looked so lonely and sad I went down to join him, and we talked. It made me look for him regularly, and we got together several times during my last year in high school."

"Did you tell Link about that?"

"I may have mentioned it when we got talking about not being able to sleep after a job. We both went through that regularly, I guess. That wasn't just when he was driving me back to the apartment the night he tried to do me. We had talked lots of times during intermissions before that."

"Who else knew you met David down by the river? You ever tell your brother, Barry?"

Her eyes narrowed. "Did he tell you I had?"

I shook my head.

"Well, I never told him. We hardly ever have talked about much of anything since our folks got killed in that accident. We talk about Grandpa and Grandma, and he's asked me about singing with the band, that's about it."

I guessed that she imagined Barry would be jealous of a rival little brother and would put him down if she ever mentioned their get-togethers.

"So," I said, "has Barry ever happened to see you wandering outside at wild hours?"

"How would he? He doesn't live close, and I've never told him I did it. Anyway, I never did that as a regular thing, you know. It's been real seldom."

"You ever see Gunnar going to work?"

"No."

"Okay, so what does that leave us with?"

"I don't know what you're trying to get at."

"Who did in Link, what else? Somebody did it. We know David was in the area, you were around, if only in your room, which I understand is on the first floor. Since David's a little too small to toss anybody anywhere, he doesn't seem too likely for it, but who knows, maybe all he had to do was trip the guy if he was in the right spot."

"That's ridiculous."

"Okay, I won't argue with you on that. But there's this big trouble with the fact that Link was out there, and nobody admits having seen or heard him. We just know that Barry and Gunnar were up and about at that time of the morning. Did one or both of those guys spot Link trying to make out with somebody, and move in on him?"

"I keep telling you, Barry doesn't live by us. He has a room closer to town."

"How much closer?"

"A few blocks. What difference does it make? Nothing would get him to come wandering out to our place at that time of morning."

"If he saw Link drive by in his fancy car, I don't doubt a minute he'd head for the Bacon place to see if that was where he was headed. If that happened, it's not at all unlikely the pair would have got in his face if he did show up. And if they met him, he was probably drunk and belligerent."

"That's too far-fetched," she said, shaking her head angrily. "It's pure nonsense."

"No more far-fetched than the plain fact that he went over that cliff and died. Or do you think he was so broken-hearted about not making you that he went out there and killed himself just to make you feel guilty?"

She scowled at me and said now I was just being snotty.

"Okay, but there's still another angle. Maybe he wasn't coming around there to see you at all. Maybe he was after Ida. Would he have learned of Gunnar's working hours that night he sat in with you, Ida, and David?"

She shook her head impatiently. "I just can't imagine him getting all excited about Ida—it's too ridiculous—"

"But it's not impossible. You already told me you saw the two of them talking by the bandstand the night he met her."

She started to smile, sensed that might be the wrong attitude, and managed another scowl. "Well, I don't suppose it'd be impossible. Barry might've told Gunnar if he'd seen us all together that evening and guessed that Link was going to try something with Ida. God knows, Gunnar would be more than able to handle Link."

"Especially if he had Barry to help."

"You keep trying to drag Barry into this. Come on, Gunnar

wouldn't need any help—or ask for it. He's big and mean enough to manage it, and if he caught Link out there and Link had been foolish enough to get snotty, I don't doubt for a second Gunnar would've gone after him. But what about the gunshot?"

"I'm glad you asked—what about it? Were you asleep when it went off?"

"Yes—it made me jump so bad the bed squeaked."

"So you were sound asleep until then?"

"Of course—"

"Then what? Did you get up? And how about your grandad—did he get out of bed and come down?"

"No. He takes off his hearing aid at night and wouldn't hear anything. Grandma just thought she'd dreamed it all and went back to sleep."

Hazel said let's drop the whole business and eat breakfast, and that's how it went.

I t was still well before lunchtime when the band gang came
around on their motor-powered raft and picked up Kat for
a rehearsal session, which they planned to hold while making
their way back to town for fresh supplies. Tipsy claimed he could
conduct and pilot at the same time.

As soon as they were off, making music before they were
twenty feet from our shore, I suggested to Hazel that we climb
the hill and visit Ida Olson before her husband got home. She
gave me a wise look, went to put on her shoes, and moments later
we were in the canoe and crossing the small span of water before
the steep bank.

"Don't tell me why we're doing this," said Hazel as we scrambled up the path. "Let me guess. You've got a notion that we
might find Link's car in that shed by the Olson house. Right?"

"You're psychic."

"As long as I'm not psychotic. You really think Gunnar's dumb
enough to leave something that dangerous in his own yard?"

"I'm not that impressed by his smarts—but probably not. I'd
just feel damned dumb if later on somebody else found it there."

The hill was no easier to climb than before. A gentle breeze moved leaves in trees along the bluff edge, and then we were walking the path between Gunnar's vegetable gardens and approaching the white clapboard house, which, I noticed, had been fairly recently painted—from the look of it, probably by an amateur who skimped.

I knocked, heard immediate footsteps, and then Ida was there beyond the screen. The light wasn't good enough to show us her expression, but when she said, "Well, hello!" there was only a hint of surprise in her voice.

"Hope we're not interrupting anything," I said. "We'd like to talk with you again if you've got the time."

She said she had all the time in the world, shoved the door open, and asked if we'd like coffee. We said not to bother, and of course she said nonsense, it was no bother, so the offer was accepted and moments later we were sitting at her small table in the narrow kitchen, sampling her fresh doughnuts. They were puffier than Ma's, and coated with powered sugar.

Ida said she was a little surprised we showed up without David because he had gone fishing and she suspected his real target was our camp and Kat. Then she asked, very casually, where Kat might be.

Hazel told her. She nodded thoughtfully and patted her hair.

"Could David swim over to their camp?" I asked.

"Oh, yes," she nodded, "he could easily do that. He's very good in the water. But he wouldn't try it because he'd be embarrassed to show up there with no really good excuse but wanting to see Kat. And he's not that crazy about those band fellas." She made a face. "I'm afraid he's awfully jealous of the whole crowd."

"He ever think of taking up a horn or something?" asked Hazel.

"Oh, I'm sure he's thought about it. But he's smart enough to know that it'd take a long time for him to become good enough to compete with any of them, and a boy his age isn't good at thinking far ahead. Nothing counts but later today, or just maybe, tomorrow."

I asked what they used their shed for. My abrupt switch away from her son got me a blank look, then a frown. "Well, it's a storage place now. Back in Gunnar's father's day, they stabled a couple horses there. Why'd you ask?"

"You don't have a car?"

"No, we don't. There's no need. Why are you asking?"

"There's a car missing. The one owned by the guy who went over the cliff here. Could somebody have hidden it out there without your knowing?"

Her face slowly reddened. "You want to go out and look? Go ahead, nobody's stopping you."

"He's not trying to be cute," said Hazel, "it's just that this is so logically the closest place it might be. If the shed's not locked, anyone could have hidden the car in there."

"So go look."

The shed had no car in it, but there was plenty of room for one on the right-hand side. Very faint tracks were barely visible on the packed dirt floor, and I couldn't tell how recent they might be. On the left-hand side the old feeding stalls were still fastened to the wall, with the giant keyhole-like openings that the horses had poked their heads through for their grain. I went back outside, staring at the ground. It was too dry and packed to show any signs clearly, but it seemed possible a car had been here at least briefly on the early morning of the murder.

"Well," said Ida brightly when I returned to the house, "did you find the man's car there with the ghosts of horses?"

"No car, no ghosts," I said. "But just let me ask one more question. Have you been gone from the house for any length of time since the morning Link died?"

"I've been shopping for groceries, yes. You think I live like a nun?"

"Never had any such notion. Does Barry come around here much?"

"You said there was only going to be one more question."

"This isn't a question, just conversation."

"All right. Yes, he comes around. Why do you ask?"

"Just wonder how well you know him, how close he and Gunnar might be. I guess they've been working together at the bakery for a quite a while."

"Its been about three years. They're used to each other. Get together and play cribbage a lot, sometimes play pool downtown. They don't talk all that much."

"I understand you met the Linklater guy a while back. When you and David were in a café with Kat."

She looked me straight in the eye. "That's right. What'd Kat tell you about that?"

"Not a lot, but she said it was plain he was really interested in you."

"That's silly. I'm almost old enough to have been his mother." She said that with a grin that made me think she was anything but offended.

"You ever see him again?"

"Where'd I see him? I never went around anyplace the band was playing after that one night."

"Well, from all we've been hearing, Link was the kind of guy who'd follow up on a lady that gave him ideas. There had to be some reason he was hanging around in your neighborhood, and from everything I've been picking up, it's hard to believe he expected to make out with Kat. Since he'd talked with you, it's easy to figure he'd heard your husband started work at four in the morning and since Link had a habit of boozing and girling after a dance job, he might have been hopped up enough to figure maybe he could find you alone about that time. What were you and Gunnar fighting about that Monday morning?"

"Oh God, who knows?" she said with a shrug. "There was always something. I guess I'd forgot to buy eggs on Saturday, and he was having a fit because he couldn't have a couple fried for his breakfast. You can be blamed sure we weren't arguing about that band man."

"When you make breakfast, have you already dressed for the day?"

She scowled at me. "Why're you asking that? What're you getting at?"

"Just trying to get the picture. After your husband goes to work, what do you usually do?"

"The dishes. What else?"

"What time does David come down for breakfast?"

"When he wakes up, which in the summer is when I go call him, around eight."

"Does he ever show up earlier when you and your husband have been having a scrap?"

"No. He stays in his room when we yell. It embarrasses him."

"So what happens—he just waits around until you come up and get him?"

"That's right."

"And that's what happened the morning of the murder?"

She stared at me, glanced at Hazel, then back at me. She reached forward, took a sip of coffee, and leaned back with exaggerated calmness while smiling thinly. "As a matter of fact, that morning after Gunnar left, it was a little different. I just went back to bed. Didn't get up till after ten. By then David had fixed his own orange juice, eaten his bran flakes, and gone for a walk."

"You sure he didn't get up and take a walk while you were fighting?"

She studied me for a long moment.

"Don't tell me—you think our thirteen-year-old boy went out and threw that man over the cliff?"

"Nope, never had any such notion. But he might've seen something if he did go out. If you and your hubby were scrapping, you wouldn't have noticed. And he might have been leery about admitting to you he'd snuck out."

"I'd have noticed," she said flatly, and got up to fetch the coffeepot.

I considered asking her if Link hadn't tried to make a date with her after Kat had left them at the café, and gone back to work, but it was clear she wasn't about to give anything away and risk having Gunnar learn about her flirting at the dance.

"Didn't David say anything to you about hearing the shot or the man screaming when he went off the cliff?" asked Hazel, as Ida refilled her cup.

"No. How'd he know anything about that?"

"I guess," said Hazel, "from the way we could hear it clear down by the river, it didn't seem likely that anybody in the neighborhood could have missed it."

"Well, you were outside, and we were in. Even with windows open, you don't hear as well from inside a house. Besides, by then, if David had been awake earlier, he was probably back to sleep while I was busy doing dishes."

There was a little more pointless talk, and finally we left and made a trip around the area. There were few houses nearby, just a couple south of the Olsons, and I looked for garages, barns, or shacks where the car might be hidden. Nothing looked promising. The woods were fairly dense, and I considered a survey on foot but had doubts about the practicality of that notion. It seemed likely that if anyone had originally hidden the car in Olson's shed, he would have moved it well away from the immediate neighborhood the first dark night after.

I finally decided the hell with it, and we headed back to our canoe.

30

We ate lunch back on the island, which Hazel decided needed a name. She suggested we call it "Honeymoon." "I'd rather call it 'Hazel's,' " I said.

"That wouldn't be right, it belongs to both of us. How about we just call it 'Our Island'?"

Later we ate lunch while talking about Ida, Gunnar, and David. That didn't get us very far, beyond agreeing that the family probably had a lot of secrets they were keeping from each other. I moved the discussion back to considerations of Link and whether or not he could really have killed Nate Pryke, which was, after all, our main problem.

Finally we dropped the whole business and went fishing. We were just getting started and hadn't hooked so much as a snag when Barry showed up, using a double-bladed paddle to guide a duck boat down the river. Hazel gave me a raised-eyebrow look before we both reeled in our lines and waded up on the beach as he pulled in. He sat a moment, looking around. He was wearing deep maroon swimming shorts, and we could see his square shoulders and muscular arms as he perched the paddle across the bow and scowled at me. "I want a talk with you," he said. It sounded like a threat.

"Fine," I said. "You mind if we keep fishing?"

"Yeah, I do. The stuff I want to cover is just between us men. Get in with me, and we'll take a little ride to get things sorted out."

"We can do it right here."

He shook his head. "This is strictly between you and me. Leave her out of it."

I looked at Hazel, who studied him and frowned.

"What's the matter," sneered Barry, still glowering at me, "you chicken?"

"I'll go with him," I told her. "It won't be for long."

She didn't like it but said nothing as I walked to the boat, climbed over the bow, and took the seat there, facing Barry. He shoved off and let the current take us downstream slowly. When we were beyond Hazel's hearing, he said, "I hear you were snooping around Olson's place earlier today—while Gunnar and I were working."

I couldn't think of anything profound to offer for that and just nodded.

"You got her all shook up," he said, and made it sound accusing.

"I'm sorry. But it was necessary."

He kept glaring at me and paddled as though he were punishing the river. "She got the notion," he said, "that you figure there's something going on between her and me. Where'd you get that crazy idea, and what the hell business is it of yours anyway?"

"I got it from talking with lots of people. And my business is finding out everything that might have any bearing on the killing. In the case of a murder, all kinds of facts can work around to an answer of who did what."

"Okay, so you were pumping Kat too. Now I got some real news for you. If you don't just back up your gear and get your ass out of this territory, I'm gonna kick your teeth out. You get the picture?"

"It doesn't focus too well. And it begins to give me real ideas about how come Link went over that cliff—it might even tell me who did in Nate too."

"You're full of shit." He cut into the water with the paddle, sending us up on a small island's beach, put the paddle down, and climbed out. I got out on the opposite side of the duck boat and watched him circle the bow toward me. Obviously he didn't think he needed any paddle for a club to settle my hash. "Okay, snoop," he snarled, "you asked for it."

He went into a crouch, feinted a left hook, then ducked his head and dove for my gut. I slipped away, bringing my right hand down in a slice that caught the back of his neck and dropped him. He rolled swiftly, expecting me to try and land on him with both feet. Instead I let him get up.

"This isn't going to get you anywhere, Barry," I said. "Even if you managed to stomp me out, what the hell is that going to do to make you look innocent?"

Not in any mood for discussion, he came at me. The sand was soft enough to make footing treacherous and I moved to my right, up toward more solid ground, as he kept coming. I've taken on a hell of a lot of scrappers over the years, but I can't remember one with more dexterity and determination. He kept moving toward me, more cautious now, but steaming. I faked a stumble and, as he threw himself at me, dropped to my back and doubled up my legs as he came down. I'd hoped to catch him in the belly, but he twisted so I only hit his chest with one foot, which spun and dropped him far to my right. When he came up, I was on my feet and caught him with a spearing left jab to the belly and a solid right hook to the jaw. He stumbled to his knees, and I caught him with a judo chop to the back of his neck.

That flattened him. I stood back and waited for him to get up. He was in no hurry. At last he rolled over slowly, sat up, and put his arms around his knees. "Jesus," he whispered, "you gotta be the dirtiest fighter I ever took on."

"Well, I'm littler than you, I can't afford to be sweet about it all."

He groaned and touched the back of his neck cautiously. "Where'd you get the duck boat?" I asked him.

"It's Gunnar's—why?"

"Just wondered. Where was Gunnar when Ida told you about our visit?"

He stretched out on his back and stared at the blue sky. "Gunnar's playing pool downtown. Your little visit got Ida so shook up she telephoned me soon's I got home to my place and told me about it."

"You ever meet Nate Pryke?"

"I suppose you got that from Kat."

"No, hadn't heard it from anybody—just wondered. Especially since you didn't mention anything about meeting him when you told us a little about him a few days ago."

He sat up painfully and stared across the smooth dark river a moment before meeting my eyes. "Okay, so I met him once. Over half a year ago. He and his wife were at a dance in town. I danced a round with her—she was something else, you know? I mean, she shoved it right up against me on the dance floor. Never knew anybody else like her. It was enough to give me a hell of a hard-on, that shook me up because I was sure folks would see. That was before I knew she was married. Never thought of looking to see if she had a ring when I asked her to dance. At the end of our round I asked how'd she like to come out to my car for a drink. She laughed real easy and said she'd like it a lot, but folks would talk because she had a husband, so she'd better not. I asked did he ever dance with her, and she said no, he didn't like dancing, but he knew she did and let her have a good time."

I asked how he'd happened to meet Nate if he hadn't been with her at the dance.

"Ran into them after the dance in the beer parlor. Talked a little. He didn't say much. Weird kind of a guy."

"And that's the only time you met him?"

"That's right."

"So, did you find out her hubby didn't like screwing either, but didn't mind if she found outside help?"

He frowned. "What I found out was, she only took on guys that blew horns or beat drums. He didn't tell me that, I heard it from guys around the dance hall. It was a big let-down."

"I guess you don't have a lot of trouble finding other lays."

He shrugged, modestly. "I get my share. Is it as much fun when you're married?"

"That all depends on who you marry. How much older than Ida is her husband Gunnar?"

"Now why'd you want to know that?"

"Nosy. That's my whole racket. I'd guess she's a lot closer to your age than his."

"You got a nasty, suspicious mind. Okay, I never asked, because it makes no difference. Hell, even if I did get ideas, Gunnar and I work the same hours—how'd you figure I'd get anywhere trying to fiddle her?"

"One thing I've learned, Barry, is that when the urge comes on, pairs always seem to find a way. And I haven't heard a word about you having any steady woman of your own."

"I love 'em all, can't settle for one."

"That's about what I figured. You and Gunnar ever talk

about his kid David and your sister? I hear he gets sore about Kat and his boy being so chummy. He ever try to talk you into telling her to lay off?"

"That's crazy. Old Gunnar hasn't the imagination to figure a gal like Kat would get hot for a kid like David. Hell, she could have any guy she ever met if she wanted him—why settle for a punk? Where the hell'd you get such a dumb notion?"

"Your sister. And she didn't figure Gunnar really believed they were doing it, but thought he was dumb enough to be suspicious."

"Oh boy, you must've really pumped her, huh? Bet you wished you had her alone, right?"

"You won't believe me, but the notion never came to mind. And she never told me you were making out with Ida; she just let me know Ida probably had a thing for you."

"Yeah, like all the girls but Carmen."

"It bother you that Carmen flirted with Link?"

"I don't know she did. How'd I know that, and if I did, what the hell would that be to me?"

"You already said she got you worked up. I'd think her going for a guy like Link would burn you pretty good. As for how you knew, maybe Kat told you."

He gave me a cold look and said they didn't gossip about the band. He had never wanted to hear any of that, and she knew it.

I heard a sound on the river and looked out to see Hazel, paddling our canoe toward us. She took in the scene and didn't quite smile.

"Here comes my wife," I told Barry. "I figure you and I are finished, so why don't you paddle back to Ida's?"

He gave me a dirty look but got up and walked a little unsteadily to the duck boat. Hazel let the canoe drift as he got in and shoved off. He didn't bother to say good-bye to either of us.

"Well," said Hazel as she pulled up on the sand, "I take it you two had a little argument. It looks like you won."

"It wasn't easy. I'm beginning to think I'm too old for his kind of waltzing."

She wanted to know all about our hassle, and I gave her a brief rundown.

She shook her head and said I was blamed lucky he hadn't simply taken after me with the paddle.

"Yeah, well, he had the notion he could do fine without it."

"Foolish boy. Now I'll tell you what I suspect."

"Shoot."

"I think he wanted you to believe there was something between him and Ida, because that could distract you from the idea he might have had something going with Carmen."

"How do you figure?"

"Okay. How could Ida and Barry get to bedding each other when Barry and her husband have identical working hours? When would they manage anything more than a little smooching?"

"You never heard that sex will find a way? And have you already forgotten I told you that he told me Gunnar was off playing pool? If Gunnar plays pool enough, that'd give Barry and Ida time for their own games."

She thought that over and allowed I might have a point. Then she asked if I thought he lied when he said Carmen only messed with band men.

"Probably."

"Yeah," she nodded, "so do I."

31

That night the band barge didn't deliver Kat until after ten. Hazel and I had taken refuge from the evening mosquitoes by ducking into our tent and, after going two rounds in the sack, were about to drift off when we heard the barge's approach, which was anything but sneaky. There was a lot of kidding around and a few laughs out on the beach before loud good-byes and the sound of the motor revving up as it headed out, and then the singer pulled aside the mosquito netting and slipped into our tent. Hazel greeted her and asked if she wanted a light. She said no thanks.

"We had a visit from your brother this afternoon," I said.

The rustle of clothing being removed stopped momentarily.

"He came *here*?" Her voice almost squeaked. "Why?"

"Wanted to talk about the visit Hazel and I had with Ida before lunch." She went on with her preparations for bed. The tent was too dark to see anything, and I didn't even try.

"Why'd you go see Ida?" she asked, trying to sound casual.

"For one thing, I wanted to check if somebody stashed Link's car in their shed."

"What a weird idea. So what'd you find?"

"It was empty. We asked her a few questions about how well she'd gotten to know Link. She claimed not at all. Also claimed she didn't give Barry any ideas, and they hadn't messed around."

"Well, what'd you expect? That she'd confess she took him to bed?"

"Actually I got the feeling she felt a little flattered that anybody would get such ideas."

Kat was silent as she slipped into her bedroll. After a few moments she asked if Barry had been mad at me because of our visit with Ida. I allowed he hadn't seemed all that pleased, but didn't mention our tussle. Then I casually told her I'd asked him whether he'd known Nate Pryke.

There was a brief silence before she asked how come I'd asked that.

"Well, Barry strikes me as a guy who likes to ask questions, and I think, given the chance, he'd try to get Nate figured out. He'd wonder why the hell this guy let his wife go to dances and didn't even hang around to make sure she behaved herself. Things like that. You ever see Nate and Barry together?"

She said no, she hadn't, and now she was tired and didn't want to talk anymore.

In the small hours I became conscious of a rumble in the distance, then there was a spattering of rain on the tent, a flash of light, and a clap of thunder that about lifted me off the ground. Hazel reached over for me and hung on while more thunder boomed and crackled.

"Oh, God," whispered Kat, "I hope that didn't hit the band raft."

"More likely it hit our island, given the time lapse between the lightning and thunder," I said.

Rain fell so hard the drumming almost matched the thunder,

which slowly began moving off. It was all clear overhead when I crawled from my sack a little later and went outside for a look around. The island was small enough to tour it easily in a few moments, and at the southern tip I found a cottonwood, half stripped of bark on one side, where the lightning had struck. There were fallen branches scattered below. I was grateful we'd not been camping under there.

Hazel was up by the time I got back to our campsite. She said Kat was still sleeping, so we should be quiet. I asked her if she believed Kat's claim that she'd not seen Barry talking with Nate. She wasn't sure but suspected, from Kat's voice, that she was probably afraid to admit it if she had, since she figured I'd pass the word to her brother in the course of a follow-up.

Hazel and I ate breakfast, then went fishing under the clear blue sky for a while without any great luck. She hooked a small bass, and I got two dinky perch, which we released. It was after ten when we got back to the camp and found Kat just finishing her breakfast fruit.

She told me she'd like to be taken over to the band's camp. She was planning to go back to her grandparents' home for Saturday night, and would take her things with her for the weekend.

So that's how it went.

When we arrived at their camp, the guys were busily uncovering the piano and drums and spreading the tarps out to dry in the sun. I talked awhile with Tipsy and managed a session with Dutch Haar, asking how often they'd spotted Barry around when they played in Wisconsin, and whether they had ever seen him in conference with Nate Pryke. Tipsy said he didn't waste any time watching guys, it was the girls that got his attention whenever he could spare it from the band. Dutch said yes, he had seen them together at least once. They seemed to be deep in discussion, and he'd wondered what in the world they had to talk about.

He decided it had to be about Kat. She always got guys talking. Or maybe it'd been about Carmen, since Barry had just been dancing with her.

"Was this in Indeville?" I asked Haar.

"Yeah. The first time we did a job there."

"You think Nate might've been getting on him about the way he'd been dancing with Carmen?"

"Not likely. In the first place, the way it looked to me, Barry was doing most of the talking. And far as I know, Nate never had anything to say to anybody about them dancing with his wife. Most of the time he didn't hang around at all. Come to think of it, that's the only time I ever remember seeing him around after he first delivered her."

I asked Haar which of the guys had told Kat about Link's bragging that he'd laid her. He looked at me a second before asking why I wanted to know that.

"Because I want to know if she actually got told that story."

"You can believe her," he said after a second. "I was the one who told her about it. I thought she ought to know what he was saying about her."

"How'd she react?"

"Well, how'd you think? She was real upset. I thought she was going to cry."

He didn't elaborate on that any, and I gave him up.

My attempt to get Skinny Engen into a private conference didn't come off. It seemed pretty evident he was avoiding me. I couldn't figure whether he'd decided he'd told me too much before, or had been warned off by other members of the band.

Maybe it was both.

When they began rehearsing, Hazel suggested we leave, and that seemed like the best idea for the time.

Nobody asked us to hang around as we headed out.

W e had a small lunch around noon, and afterward neither of us was in a fishing mood. Hazel suggested we go around to the Bacon place again.

"What've you got in mind?" I asked.

She shrugged and said she just felt like talking with Cole. That's all she'd say about it, so we climbed the hill once more, crossed the now-familiar area where Link had begun his flight, and found Katerina Bacon pulling weeds in her backyard vegetable garden.

She greeted us warmly and said she hoped that Kat was having a good time and did not get in our way. We assured her all was well. She accepted that with enough grace to suggest she realized how inhibiting the guest would be on a honeymoon, but was not about to start any discussion of the subject. And of course we went along when she suggested we go inside and share a cup of coffee with her and Cole.

The old man greeted us from his easy chair in the corner and asked, with only a hint of sarcasm, if the sheriff had his murder case all wrapped up.

"Not that I know of."

"About what I'd expect with him. He don't know shit from Shinola but never shines his shoes, so it don't make no never-mind. How about you, Hobo Cop, you gonna catch the villain?"

"I haven't even been able to catch any good fish," I admitted.

He grinned. "Mebbe you come to the wrong river."

"It's not the river that gives us our problems. In fact, if we'd just stayed on it, life would be a hell of a lot less complicated. I've been wondering, didn't Kat ever bring any of her band friends around your place?"

"What for? We ain't got no dance floor, nor piano. What'd that bunch of night crawlers want around here?"

"I'd expect a guy like you would want to know what kind of a crowd your granddaughter was working with. Didn't you ever ask her to bring them around?"

He shifted in his easy chair and peered at me with his watery blue eyes sparkling. "Matter of fact, she did invite 'em around a coupla times. I never gave her any crap about bringing friends home. That's the way I want it, so's I can keep at least a half an eye on things. Besides, those guys weren't in this territory that often, so I never figured they'd get to be any big nuisance."

"You ever figure she had any favorites in that bunch?"

"Hah! If she did, she'd never let any of 'em know it. That's always been her style, since her last year in high school. Keep 'em all panting."

"You have a favorite for her?"

"Well, if she was gonna favor any of 'em, I'd have picked the Dutchman, Haar. He wasn't pushy, and he could be starry-eyed about Kat without making a damn fool of himself."

I asked Cole when he had quit farming.

"It was eight year ago this spring. Katarina's cousin, old Judge Cannon, didn't have no living kin but her, so when he croaked he left this house and a nice bundle to my ever-lovin' wife. It took me about thirty seconds to figure we had all we needed of fighting bugs, contrary weather, and general farming grief, and I just folded up the whole damned business, sold the old farmhouse and land, and moved in here. Timing was perfect. The depression hadn't hit yet, and prices for land were still fair. Kat was tickled pink. Instead of hiking near a mile to school, she walked a few blocks, and there was even more kids to play with than she'd had around when she was little and livin' in town with her ma and pa before their accident."

"She like school?" Hazel asked.

"Loved it," said Katarina. Her broad face seemed even wider when she smiled. "She was always a teacher's pet in every grade, and I guess the most popular girl in her class. You know that doesn't happen often—I mean, usually kids hate anybody the teachers go for. But Kat's always made everybody love her."

I thought I could catch a hint of cynicism in the old man's eye, and guessed that he, like me, had serious doubts about how universally loved any girl as good-looking and talented as Kat would be with her girl classmates.

"She ever bring kids home?" asked Hazel.

"No," said Cole, before his wife could speak.

"Not girls or boys?"

"Nope. Kids around here just don't do that, starting about when they get into junior high. From then on the whole business with other kids in school is separate from home."

I knew that was especially true with farm kids. Most of them went home from school and on to chores. They didn't have time for much fooling around except Saturday nights, though a few had Sundays free and then they just wanted to get away from family and enjoy classmates without adult intrusion.

I asked Cole for his impressions of the band guys who

showed up. He admitted, rather grudgingly, that they were generally okay. He remembered the names of Chris and Tipsy, but wasn't sure of the others except for Dutch Haar. He didn't mention Link at all, and when Hazel asked what he had thought of him, the old man just shrugged as if he'd not been much noticed.

Hazel admired the crocheted arm covers she noticed on Cole's easy chair and asked Katarina if she also did knitting and other handcrafting. That got Katarina going in great shape, and she wound up taking Hazel for a stroll through the house to show off her handiwork. I asked Cole if he'd like to go outside and share a smoke with me. He said why not? As we strolled across his front lot, he accepted one of my prerolled cigarettes and the light I offered.

He talked some, saying again that he was grateful to have missed the grief common with all farmers in our territory who were still hanging on. He had suspicions about the Roosevelt administration in general and the president in particular. Too big a smile, too long a cigarette holder, too handy with the fancy phrases and general bullshit. When I questioned him some, it came out that he hadn't liked Hoover either, and had in fact voted for FDR. Plainly, Cole was simply unable to accept any man in power or even close to it. This got me thinking a little about my own attitudes in that line.

Cole admitted a particular interest in the death of Nate Pryke and a strong suspicion that it was not suicide. When asked about his neighbor Gunnar, he shook his head.

"Hardly ever see him and never heard anything about him that made it seem worthwhile trying to get acquainted. What can you expect of a man who gets up at three in the morning every working day? I got the feeling he ain't got brains enough to pour piss out of a boot if they was directions on the heel. And if he had any sense at all, he'd know that wife of his was messing with Barry."

"Why'd he think that?"

"Because the kid's a born tail-chaser, and she's younger than her husband and hotter than a branding iron."

"She ever make a pass at you?"

"Of course. At least once a week. And if you believe that, I got a gold mine I'll sell you cheap. How long you been married?"

"Near three weeks."

"How long since you first met her?"

"Maybe six months."

"She learn to ask questions from you, or is she just a born quizzer?"

"Hazel's never needed anybody to tell her what to do or how to do it."

"Uh-huh. That's easy to believe. You're pretty lucky, eh? Got a great-looking woman and a smart partner to boot, right? Can she cook?"

"You bet."

"If I wasn't such an old fart, I'd be envious."

"I don't think you're that old, but just between us characters, I've a strong hunch you've been holding out on me."

His eyebrows went up, and the grin broadened.

"Now why'd I hold out on you? I figure we see eye to eye pretty regular."

"You've got a shotgun, haven't you?"

"That's no big secret."

"Okay. So I've been holding out on you. What I really think is, you learned about Link's coming on to Kat. Maybe she'd even warned you he might be coming around. And when he did, she made a racket, you grabbed your shotgun, charged him and let go at him—maybe you just shot in the air to scare him—and it probably worked better than you expected because he panicked and went over the cliff."

He kept grinning, butted out his cigarette, and said we should go back in the house. "Your wife's probably got Katarina hoarse from gabbing."

We found the two women sitting in the bedroom on the south side of the house, chatting like a pair of old classmates. Katarina broke off when she saw her husband, got up, and suggested we have another cup of coffee. Hazel said we'd already imposed too much, and after some more polite talk, we left.

"What'd you learn from Cole?" she asked as we headed back to the island.

"He works full-time at being a character. How'd you do with Katarina?"

"I learned that the granddaughter sleeps in a bedroom off the kitchen downstairs, and Cole and Katarina have separate bedrooms upstairs. She also said Cole has trouble sleeping and gets up in the night and wanders around the house and even outside sometimes. I think you learned something from the old man— you've got a wise look."

"I told him I figured it was his shotgun that sent Link over the cliff. He just looked smug and suggested we go back in the house. Did Katarina give you any ideas?"

"Nary a one. She claims to be a heavy sleeper and didn't hear anything like a shot."

"Well," I said, "I figure Link tried climbing in Kat's window downstairs, she screamed, and the old man charged in, cut loose once, and scared him over the cliff. The hitch is, everything she's told us—and the guys have supported her—she had turned Link down cold when he tried the other time, so it just doesn't make sense he'd try sneaking in on her here. Why'd she have let him get that far after the public fuss? Maybe we could argue that she was still so mad at him for bragging to the guys about making her, she wanted to give him a real jolt and lured him into her room so her grandpa could catch him at it and raise hell. Maybe she even warned the old man to watch out for him."

Hazel couldn't quite buy that but she admitted it was probably because she really liked the old man and didn't want him to get any blame for Link's jump.

I told her I wasn't about to have anybody bring charges against him, and if anybody else did, they wouldn't be able to make a murder charge out of it if he'd just scared the guy off.

"Now all we've really got to do is get Carmen to admit she knows that Link murdered Nate Pryke."

"So we can collect from old man Pryke—right?"

"You've got it."

nstead of going back to the island, we walked into town, where we found Dewey in the sheriff's office. I gave him a rundown on our talk with Cole and his wife without mentioning my suspicions about Cole.

"So," he said, "you figure the missing Link showed up at the Bacon place, Cole caught him trying to sneak in with Kat, got his shotgun, and ran him off the cliff?"

"I wouldn't say he ran him off—but he might have fired a warning shot that did it. You know if the old man's got a gun?"

"He had one when Barry and I were buddies. Barry borrowed it when we went hunting. A four-ten. Lots lighter than a twelve-gauge. Maybe we should get a search warrant and go over their place. Might find Link's wallet."

I shook my head. "No. That old man would never frisk Link before running him off the cliff and then be dumb enough to keep the billfold."

"So who took it off the body down on the tracks?"

"You and the sheriff searched me and our stuff and didn't find it—"

"You could've stashed it in the brush somewhere, up there or even down here. There was plenty of time."

"Okay. You figure we had time enough to hide this guy's car too?"

Dewey took a deep breath and let it out slowly.

"That'd be hard to figure," he granted. "The trouble is, I just can't picture that old geezer scrambling around like a juvenile delinquent. And his wife was bound to have heard the uproar if he caught the couple in action—she sure as hell would've heard the shot and scream when Link went over—"

"So? What if she did? You think she'd feel bound to turn the old man in?"

"Of course not, but I just can't believe she could've have handled the whole thing as neat as she did, if she knew everything that happened."

Hazel shook her head. "Men always have to underestimate a country wife, or almost any other woman, for that matter. But either way, we won't get anything from her."

"Okay," said Dewey, "I'm not gonna push that. The biggest headache is still, what happened to his damned car?"

"Why don't we go visit Carmen's farm?" asked Hazel. "There must be a barn there, or maybe a shed where the car would fit."

So the three of us piled into our snappy Model A, which I'd left parked by the city hall downtown, and headed for the Pryke farm.

The sky was clear except for cirrus clouds in the north, so steady there they looked painted against the blue. The road was rough gravel most of the way until we turned off on a dirt road and approached the rise leading to the Pryke farmhouse, which stood at the hill's flat top. Compared with farmhouses familiar to me in South Dakota, this one looked brand-new. The paint was fresh, the shingles even and clean.

The fields around hadn't been farmed since Nate's death, and there was crabgrass in all directions.

We found no car in the front yard, and it wasn't surprising to get no response when we went up to the kitchen door and knocked. I looked out at the barn a few dozen yards to the north and the unpainted shack off a ways east of it.

We headed for the barn. The center door was closed but slid aside easily; inside, it smelled of dry hay and cow manure. There were no animals in sight, and the earthen floor was strewn thinly with hay. I glanced up at the loft, decided there was no point in climbing up there, and the three of us went back outside.

The shed had a southerly lean, and I suspected it had been ignored by Nate since everything else around, including the barn, must have been painted within the last two years.

The double front doors wouldn't open, but we found a narrow side one that did. It was dark inside, so much so it was hard to see the Oldsmobile until my eyes adjusted. It was parked, facing inside, just two feet beyond the big doors.

"Bingo," said Hazel.

34

The keys were in the ignition. There was nothing in the trunk but a jack and wrench. I looked under the front seat and found Link's .32 pistol. It was loaded.

I suggested we swing around to the restaurant where Carmen worked, and Hazel said fine, it was almost time for dinner anyway. Dewey was willing.

The place was almost empty when we arrived. Carmen spotted us at once from behind the counter and smiled automatically as we approached, but our faces gave her a message that sobered her.

"We've been out to your farm," said Dewey.

"You've got that wrong, it was never mine. It was always Grandpa Gideon's, and it's been up for sale ever since Nate died."

"But nobody's taken it yet, right? What do you think we found in the shed out back?"

She looked from Dewey's face to mine, then back.

"Why don't you just tell me," she said.

"We found Linklater's Oldsmobile. How you suppose it got there?"

"You going to have dinner?" she asked calmly.

I looked at Dewey, who said yes.

Carmen led us to a corner table, handed us menus, and waited. All three of us concentrated on the menus, letting her wait nervously.

"So," she said at last, "you think I threw him over the cliff, stole his car, and drove it out to the farm to keep as a souvenir?"

Dewey at first looked startled, then couldn't help grinning. I decided to butt in.

"Nobody thinks you murdered him," I said, "but come on, Carmen, you've got to admit it's damned hard for us to think you weren't involved one way or another with Link that night. You were together earlier on, weren't you?"

She sighed, looked around the almost empty restaurant, and finally slipped into a chair facing me.

"Okay," she said, "I was with Francis Sunday night. He came around and picked me up and drove me out to Arnie Arhart's place. You know about that?"

I shook my head.

"Well, it's a mostly singles bar that's unlicensed, but they let us in, and I played double solitaire with Arnie's wife, Tina, while Francis played poker with some guys. We played for a penny a point, and I had a good night, playing every card in three different games before she backed off. Francis didn't do so well but kept trying until nearly three A.M., when everybody else decided to call it quits, and we all left.

"Francis was real drunk by then, and we took a little ride, finally parked in front of my apartment. He got real pushy at petting and wanted to go further. I told him I was having my period. He made me prove it and then insisted that I do him another way and I got so mad I told him he should just go over to the Bacons' and make out with Kat. He said that was a stupid idea, but I told him no, I'd heard Kat had let him do it before and she'd be glad to do it again. More than one of the fellows in the band had told me that. At first he didn't believe me, but he was drunk enough to like the idea and said okay, he'd drive to her house and let me drive myself home if I'd bring the car back in the morning. So I went along."

"Had you really heard from the band that Kat had taken on Link?" I asked.

"Of course."

"Give us names," said Dewey.

"I can't."

"Why?" pushed Dewey.

"I promised not to tell anybody."

"Lady," he said, "this here's a murder we're dealing with. You can't just wave us off like we were nosy neighbors. You want to be accused of being an accessory to murder?"

She stared at him with her mouth sagging and her eyes moist.

"You're not going to get any of these guys in trouble by being honest with us," I told her.

She finally said she wasn't sure just which ones had told her—she guessed it had maybe been Tipsy Tobler, Nolan Watson, and Dutch Haar.

"Okay," said Dewey, "let's get back to Link. Where'd he get out of the car?"

"By the Bacons' house."

"And you're telling us you drove out to your old farm?"

"Well, I didn't have a garage at my new place, so I just took it where nobody'd see it and get ideas."

"Are you trying to make us believe you walked miles back to town after three in the morning?"

"Well, no. Actually I slept the rest of the night there, and late in the morning I called Pop from the crossroads store, and he came and got me."

Dewey stared at her, and she met his eye without flinching.

"How come you didn't keep your promise to go back and pick up Link in the morning?"

"Well, what sense would that make? There was no way of telling how long he'd be with her, if he managed at all. You think I was just going to sit around after three in the morning waiting for that idiot—especially after the way he treated me?"

"All right," said Dewey finally, "we'll check with Pop. Is he out back?"

She said yes.

Dewey looked at me. "How about you go bring him out here?" I found the old man sitting at a kitchen table, working on a menu. When I told him the deputy wanted him to answer some questions, he raised his eyebrows, but said nothing and trailed me back into the dining area.

Dewey didn't horse around—he asked him to confirm what Carmen had told us. He glanced at her and said yes, she'd called late in the morning, and he went and got her. After some more questions Dewey thanked him, let him go back to his kitchen, and then told Carmen she'd have to come to the station with us and make a formal statement.

We went to the police station and found the Foxton cop, Conklin Mertz, at his desk.

Dewey explained what was up, and they got Carmen seated and asked her to tell her whole story of the business with Link once more, how she wound up with his car and took it to the farm.

Mertz was indignant about her abandoning Link that way and wanted to make her admit she'd simply stolen the man's car.

She said she'd just wanted to get back at him for the way he treated her, and he wouldn't have had any real trouble getting his car back if he hadn't been killed trying to get away from somebody up at the Bacons' house. Finally Mertz took Dewey out of the room with him, I guessed to try and figure out a way to nail Carmen for some kind of misdemeanor.

Carmen watched the doorway, frowning nervously.

"You look really worried," said Hazel gently.

"Why wouldn't I be? Everybody wants a goat in this mess, and they haven't been able to come up with anybody else, so you're all trying to make it me. That's perfectly obvious."

"We don't. And I doubt that Dewey does. We just want to get the story straight. Why'd you tell Link that Kat would let him have her?"

She took a deep breath and sighed. "Because I hoped there'd be a big flare-up; I was plenty mad at both of them."

"How about your husband's shotgun?" asked Hazel gently.

Carmen stared at her a moment, swallowed, and finally asked what she meant by asking that question.

"Nothing we've ever heard about him suggests he was a hunter," I told her. "So we wonder, how come he had a gun around?"

She took a deep breath, trying, I felt, to calm herself. "It was a present from his uncle. He thought a farmer should have something to keep away pest animals."

"You ever see him use it?"

"Not that I remember. I mean, he didn't carry it with him when he went out to work in the fields or the barn."

"Where'd he keep it?"

"I guess it was down in the basement. I don't really remember noticing. Guns have never interested me."

"How'd he feel about you going to visit your father over that last weekend?"

"Well, he always acted a little bothered when I went to Dad's—I mean he's not a man who knew how to make his own meals, he didn't even shop much. But he wasn't suspicious about me, if that's what you're getting at."

"Did he go to town for meals?"

"No. He didn't go much of anywhere."

Hazel leaned toward her.

"Did you ever suspect he felt suicidal?"

"Not really. He'd get depressed now and then, but when he drank it seemed to take care of it."

"Did Link ever come around to the farm?" I asked.

"Never. Why in the world would he?"

"Well, we hear he was pretty involved with you—maybe he came around to see what your home life was like."

"That's dumb. It's the last thing he'd ever dream of."

"Do you think if Barry got the idea that Link was going to go around and bother his sister, he'd hunt him down and maybe even kill him?"

She shook her head. "I don't think Barry would do anything but beat him up good."

"Did Barry ever come out to your farm before your husband died?"

"No."

"How about after?"

"How would I know? After Nate died, I packed up and left and didn't go back until I took the car there."

Dewey came back to join us and asked if we'd covered all the questions we had to ask. I said there were a couple more, and he told me to go at it.

"Okay," I said, and turned back to Carmen. "Did Link ever come out to the farm when your husband was still alive?"

"No," she said, shaking her head firmly.

"Okay. Now we've got a really big problem here. How the hell did Link know that your husband had a bundle of money stashed away in the house? And before you answer—just think a bit. Nobody else could know about it if you didn't tell, could they?"

She looked flustered and didn't answer for a few seconds.

"All right," she said finally, "I did admit to him that there was money in the house. He'd made remarks about Nate being a damned fool not to be able to do anything he pleased when he had this rich uncle who could fix him up with anything at all."

"Did you know where Nate hid his stash?"

"I just assumed it was somewhere in his room. I never looked for it."

We all stared at her, and she flushed but insisted she couldn't tell us any more on that subject.

Dewey finally asked her how well she had known her neighbors, Clarence Quinn and his wife, Honoria.

"Hardly at all. Nate used to go over and talk with them a lot, but Honoria never came to our place. When Clarence did, it was just to help Nate in the fields. He was real nice that way. He came around pretty regular. Oh, I gave him coffee on days when they worked a long time together outside."

"He pay any attention to you?"

"He never made any passes, if that's what you're trying to get at. He only came around when Nate was home."

"Did Gunnar know your husband at all?" asked Hazel.

Carmen looked at her and frowned. "How would he? From what Barry tells me, Gunnar's always either in the back rooms of the bakery, working in his garden, or bowling. I don't guess he's ever been outside of Indeville, and probably hasn't been anyplace else but along the river, where he spends some time looking for his kid, who's always off poking around in the woods along there."

Dewey asked a few more general questions and finally gave up and told her she could go but be sure that she stayed in town.

She gave him a beaming smile, nodded at Hazel and me, and left.

35

azel and I left the police station, and she suggested we go the café for a cup of coffee.

I took my first sip and leaned against the booth back. "Why do I have this sneaky feeling that you've got a new idea about our little case here?" I asked.

She grinned. "Because you're psychic with me."

"More like psycho—but what's the pitch?"

She leaned forward. "I've been thinking for several days about why Nate was so liberal in sharing his wife with all of the guys in the band and maybe some dancers to boot. And that started me thinking about what might have been going on between him and his farmer neighbor, Clarence, who was so eager to help him work his farm."

My mouth didn't exactly drop open, but whatever my expression was, it tickled Hazel. She smiled tolerantly. "I guess you haven't known any homos," she said.

"I heard of them in the big house and the army, but never knew any guys like that. I suspect there's never been one in South Dakota."

"Oh, sure. But we're in Wisconsin, in case you've forgotten."

"Well, sure. But what the hell—Clarence and Hon had a baby—"

"Maybe it wasn't his. But more than likely it was, and he's just ambisextrous."

My jaw must have dropped, because she started laughing and asked if I'd never heard of that term before. I had to admit I hadn't. After some thought, I decided she might be on the right track.

We finished our coffee, paid for it, went out to the Model A, and climbed in. "All right," I said, "we'll go visit the Quinns."

The sun was hot, and the howling wind made the car shudder on the graveled road. "How are you going to handle this?" Hazel asked.

"I'm not sure. Just play it by ear, I guess."

The porch seemed even more saggy than the last time we'd been around. I parked about a dozen feet from the stone path, and the chubby Hon appeared behind the screen door, pushed it open, and stepped outside to greet us with a combination of polite welcome and curiosity.

"You're too late for dinner," she said, "but I could offer you dessert."

Hazel grinned, thanked her, and said we'd just dropped around to chat and offered to help do the dishes if she hadn't finished the job.

"My, how thoughtful. Actually I've already done them. But come on in—I'll fix us some coffee."

The baby, Nelly, was in her basket on the floor between the kitchen table and the stove.

"Where's Clarence?" I asked as we sat down at the table.

"Out in the barn. Somehow he always saves chores for after dinner—when he was a boy, his mother made him help dry dishes after meals, and one of the first understandings we had when we married was that he wouldn't help with that job."

She smiled at me and asked if I wanted to call Clarence inside.

"Don't bother, you and Hazel gossip lady-style, and I'll go out and gas with your hubby, man to man," I said.

Clarence was sitting on a bale of hay near the open door of the barn, a large gray-and-white cat parked in his lap. They both observed my approach with interest if not any particular welcome until I was close. Then Clarence grinned and told the cat this fellow was the detective from South Dakota. He placed the cat on the floor and got up. "So," he said, "what can I do for you, Detective Wilcox?"

"You could call me Carl, for one thing."

He showed his good teeth in a broad grin and said, "Okay, Carl. How come you're out in the country this evening?"

"Like to talk to you a little more about Nate Pryke."

He produced a package of Old Golds, offered me one, and when I took it, lit us both up.

"Okay," he said, exhaling casually, "what do you want to know?"

"From everything I've heard about Nate, it seems pretty plain he wasn't exactly a lady's man. He was married to a sexy babe but apparently never serviced her and didn't mind if she laid other guys. So I wonder, did he maybe like guys, and did he ever make a pass at you?"

He grinned at me. "You think I'd go for that?"

"Well, it doesn't seem likely, since you've got a wife and kid and seem to get on fine, but I'd like to get the whole picture of this guy clear, and so far I haven't been able to do it. From everything I've heard, Nate had nobody else around here that he talked to, and you were so willing to help him out, it seems likely he might have unloaded some on you, maybe even made a pass."

His grin broadened. "You figure I'm what they call a two-wayer?"

"I figure Nate may have hoped so."

The grin faded some. "Well, he never made any passes, and I never invited any. He just wanted all the help I could offer on his farm, and when we took breaks he liked to gab a lot."

"Okay, did you ever ask him how he felt about his wife messing around with other guys?"

He took a deep drag on his cigarette and blew it out slowly. After a moment the smile came back. "As a matter of fact, I did. I kept it casual as hell, you know, trying to make him see I was just interested in how things were for him—like a friend ought to be. He took it that way. It was almost like he'd been expecting me to ask—maybe even wanted me to. He said that he and Carmen had a complete understanding. She cooked and served the meals, took care of the house, and he kept her dressed good and didn't mind if she ran around."

"Did you really believe he didn't care if she got screwed by other guys?"

"Well, he didn't like her being too obvious about it. One time I know he told her she could try to be more of a lady and quit pushing her sex against the guys in front of everybody in the dance hall."

"That's all it came to?"

"Well, no. Lately he did get kind of browned off and told me he was thinking of giving up the farm and going someplace like Minneapolis where he could make a new life for himself, dumping both his wife and his bossy uncle all at once."

"You think he was serious about that?"

"Well, he wanted to be, but I never figured he'd have the balls to actually do it, no matter how much he dreamed about it."

"Did Carmen know anything about this notion?"

"Not likely. He knew damned well she'd squeal to the old man, and that old fart would corral him in jig time."

"Like how?"

"Damned if I know—but a guy with his kind of dough and savvy can manage just about anything he wants to."

"He didn't have much luck in helping Nate become a farmer."

He grinned and conceded the point, but said the idea of farming was originally Nate's—he figured it could make him independent eventually. He just never realized how damned much work goes into farming.

"Did you tell your wife about Nate's plan?" I asked.

"I suppose I mentioned it. She was real interested in Nate and of course had heard from church friends about how Carmen carried on. She'd been suspicious about how things were between them from the start."

"Did Nate ever talk about selling the farm?"

"Hell, he couldn't. It wasn't his to sell. The old man owns it all, lock, stock, and barrel."

"I don't suppose you ever met the old man?"

"Nope. He wasn't what you'd call a regular visitor, but when he did show, Nate never called for help, and I stayed away like I figured he wanted me to."

"Did he ever tell you about having a stash someplace—enough so he could actually make a go at living in Minneapolis if he decided to make that move?"

"Well, yeah—when I asked him how he could manage just taking off and leaving the farm. He kind of got a kick out of telling me he'd managed to build up a pretty nice bundle by bumming money from the old man regularly for equipment he never got around to buying. Actually I was kind of surprised that old Grandpa Gideon trusted him so much he never checked up—but hell, a guy with his kind of money doesn't have to worry about stuff like that."

"Did you ever tell your wife about this notion of Nate's?"

He grinned. "Funny you should ask. As a matter of fact, Hon asked me if Nate had ever talked about leaving the farm. She knew he was unhappy with it because I'd told her about his fight to keep it going. So she mentioned it to her lady friends, and I suppose one of them could've passed it on to Carmen. Women in town generally didn't have any love of her, and they'd figure the rumor would maybe tame her down on the flirting with every guy in town."

We talked a little more before I thanked him and headed back to the house. He was sitting down again, lighting up a cigarette and waiting for his cat to jump on his lap, as I left.

Hazel and Hon were still gabbing over coffee when I walked in. After a few more pleasantries, we said good-byes.

36

he problem," I told Hazel as we drove back toward town, "is that we may find old Gideon won't be real happy about the solution of this murder when we tell him the killer is dead and the death was probably accidental."

"You think we should work out a way where we can convince him you polished Link off?"

"That'd sure fix it up for us, but I don't think even you are cagey enough to pull that off. I'm convinced Link killed Nate. We've got to talk with Dewey and find out exactly how Nate was posed for the suicide shot. The way I figure, the trigger had to be tripped by the thumb to be believable for a suicide. What was the position of the gun when they first found him?"

We found Dewey where I expected to, in the local café. He greeted us with his usual enthusiasm about a chance to rubberneck at Hazel, and I got straight to the point.

"Who was the cop that went to check up on the shooting Quinn reported when he went to Nate's farm that night?"

"Me."

"Did you figure it was suicide from the start?"

"It pretty much looked that way. The body had fallen off the bench; the rifle, a Springfield Model 15 single-shot, was between his legs. The shell was a long rifle .22. There were smeared fingerprints on it, but they didn't tell me anything. If he actually did shoot himself, he'd have used his thumb on the trigger, and the shock of the lead between his eyes probably would've messed up the print. We couldn't make any conclusions about that. The fact that there were no fingerprints on the stock or barrel made me suspect the thing had been wiped clean."

"So it's pretty likely, isn't it, that Link shot him and then set the scene for a suicide?"

"I figure it was either him or Carmen. And since Carmen's old man has sworn she was with him, there's not much chance of making a case against her."

"Well, just between us guys, I'd a lot rather settle for it being Link. We don't have to worry about him coming up with an alibi at this stage. But where does that leave us with the question of how Link went over the cliff?"

"I don't really give a damn about that question. Perfectly willing to call it an accident, since he was drunker than a skunk, it was a dark night, and nobody stands out as a suspect that anybody around here is gonna make a big deal of it."

"You think your boss will settle for that?"

"Hell, yes. He's not gonna get half the town on his ear by trying to pin anything on old man Bacon, let alone the local dream girl."

After a little more talk, Hazel suggested we drift, and we said our good-byes.

"So what've you got in mind," I asked when we were out on the street, "maybe a little powwow with Cole Bacon and his granddaughter?"

"Weren't you thinking about that?"

"Uh-huh. Who knows, if the old man will confess to firing the shot that sent Link out of this world, maybe the priceless Pryke will send them a token check for knocking off his beloved nephew."

"And maybe he'll give you the two thousand dollars he promised for a solution to this thing."

It was late enough by that time to make me think it best to approach the Coles the next day—and since that was Sunday, it'd be best after noon.

e pulled up in front of the Bacons' house just after one-thirty in the afternoon and found Cole sitting on a lounge chair, admiring the summer day while smoking a cigar. He greeted us with a certain cautious cordiality, waved us toward the outdoor couch against the front wall, and asked what brought us around.

"We're about to head back for the river and then to South Dakota," I said. "Thought we should say good-bye. Are Kat and Barry around?"

"Kat is. So what's happened—you give up on the murder, or is it all solved?"

I allowed it was solved as far as the local cops were concerned, and that was all that really counted. "But all the same," I said, "I'd like to get straight on a couple points just for personal satisfaction, since this is the first murder I've been involved in when the killer didn't get nailed."

The screen opened, and Kat came out wearing shorts, a blue blouse, and a worried frown. I was so accustomed to her entertainer's professional smile that it seemed this was someone new.

She responded overpolitely to our greeting and asked me if Dewey had sent us around.

"Nope. He's satisfied that Link's death was accidental and told me his boss wasn't about to stir up folks around here by making any accusations against you or your grandpa. As far as the local law is concerned, the whole thing is settled."

Her eyebrows climbed a skeptical notch, and her soft mouth was grim. "If that's so, why are you back here asking questions?"

"Like I told your grandpa, I'm really stumped about this whole business and want to get to the bottom of it. Everybody knows he had the hots for you, and from everything we've heard from Carmen, he was too drunk to be smart, so I figure he came to your window and either tapped on it or tried to crawl through, if it happened to be open, which it probably was on a summer night. That makes me wonder—did you grab your grandpa's gun and take a shot to scare him off—or did you really try to hit him?"

"What happened," interrupted the old man, "was that when that sonuvabitch crawled through the window, Kat yelled, and I came runnin' with my four-ten. He slicked out the window, stumbled, and fell when I pulled the trigger, and the next I knew he was hollering his way over the cliff."

"Did anybody tell you that there wasn't a single piece of buckshot in the body when it hit the tracks?" I asked.

He scowled at me. "Where'd you hear that?" I couldn't tell from his expression whether he was disbelieving or disappointed.

"Dewey. He got that straight from the medical examiner and assured us that had made the sheriff close the case."

The old man looked at Kat, who stared at me in disbelief.

"Why wouldn't Dewey tell us that when they questioned us that day?" she asked.

"There was no reason for him to tell you."

"You believe him?" Kat asked her grandpa. She suddenly looked ready to cry.

Cole sobered and examined me. Then he looked at her and nodded. "Yeah, I do. This South Dakota hick is a slicker, but he wouldn't lie in front of his wife."

Kat shook her head, swallowed hard, and came up with a handkerchief to wipe her watering eyes. Then her face turned angry. "No one told us that," she said. "They let us think he'd been hit, trying to trick us into admitting murder. That's what made Barry try to make you quit and go away and why both of us lied so much. We both thought Grandpa had killed him."

"I don't think the police tried to trick you," Hazel said gently. "It simply never occurred to them to mention it when they questioned you. In fact they may not have even had the complete report from the doctor when you were questioned."

Kat didn't look convinced, but when she looked at her grandfather he grinned and winked at her. "You got nothing to worry about, Kitten. Why don't we offer these folks a cup of coffee?"

Hazel said thanks a lot, but we should be moving on, and when I got up, the old man rose and we shook hands.

"It's been a pleasure," he said. "Hope the rest of your river trip goes good."

When we got out to our car, I suggested we call on Gideon Pryke and his sidekick, Ronald.

"You figure it's time to pick up your fee?"

"Why not?"

We found the old man at Carmen's father's home. He was on the telephone to New York when we arrived and finished up his gab shortly after we sat down with his man Rochford.

When he joined us, I explained the story of Link's death, and the conclusion reached by the local constabulary that Link had killed Nate and arranged to make it appear a suicide.

"Was Carmen involved in any way, do you think?"

"Nobody's been able to make a case of it, since her father swears she was with him that night and we've no evidence to the contrary."

He wanted all the details, and I supplied them the best I could. "Well," he said at last, "it appears that you've done your job, and nobody is going to get pinned down for the murder of the murderer. I guess there's a touch of poetic justice there. So what do you figure I owe you, one or two thousand?"

"Well, the way it all worked out, maybe you could see your way to making it fifteen hundred."

He laughed, got out his checkbook, quickly wrote a check, blew on it, and handed it over.

I stuck it in my pocket without glancing at the amount, and we shook hands. He also shook hands with Hazel, and bowed us out.

"Aren't you going to look at it?" asked Hazel as we got in the car.

"Why should I?"

"To see if it's one thousand or fifteen hundred."

"It's neither," I said. "It's two thousand."

"You peeked?"

"Only into his soul."

"Oh, cut that out—let me see."

I pulled it out of my pocket and handed it over.

"Well, I'll be damned," she said.

"Oh you of little faith," I said, and kissed her.

As we headed back for the river, I told Hazel it seemed like we could now retire and live a life of ease.

"Oh sure," she said, "but first we'll just go have the honeymoon we started out on. Only this time we'll stay well away from any railroad tracks."